LARRY

Adam Millard was born in Shrewsbury, England, in 1980, and grew up in Wolverhampton. He is the author of the zombie novels, *Dead Cells*, *Dead Frost*, and *Dead Line*, the bizarre novellas, *Zoonami*, *Hamsterdamned!* and *Vinyl Destination*, and the supernatural novels, *Deathdealers* and *The Susceptibles*. He can be contacted through www.adam-millard.com.

Also by Adam Millard

Only in Whispers
The Ballad of Dax and Yendyll
Grimwald The Great
Dead West
Dead Cells
Dead Frost
Dead Line
Deathdealers
The Susceptibles
Olly
Skinners
Divided
Chasing Nightmares
Peter Crombie, Teenage Zombie
Peter Crombie Vs The Grampires
The Secret Diary of Peter Crombie
The Marionnettiste of Versailles: and
Other Oddities
Hamsterdamned
Vinyl Destination
Zoonami

LARRY

Adam MILLARD

This Edition Published 2023 by Crowded
Quarantine Publications
The moral right of the author has been asserted

A CIP catalogue record for this book
is available from the British Library

ISBN: 978-1-7384764-1-1

Crowded Quarantine Publications
124 Dimsdale Parade West
Newcastle-Under-Lyme
Staffordshire
ST5 8DU

1
Camp Diamond Creek – 1978

The girl ran through the woods, breasts bouncing like two bowling balls in a cheaply constructed knapsack, tripping over things that most children could have knocked aside without too much effort. She was tired and terrified, and tired of *being* terrified. The nightmare seemed to be neverending, and yet it *had* ended for Billy, and Roger, and Deborah, and Kaycee, and twelve other kids that she couldn't name even if you gave her a thousand attempts.

The bastard in the creepy pig mask had killed them all.

He'd decapitated Billy with an axe. Roger had been forced through a wood-chipper, and had come out the other end looking like something you would fry with onions. Deborah and Kaycee had been getting it on in the middle of the woods, and had been just about to go down on one another when Pigface had decided to beat them both to death with Billy's severed head. The twelve other kids...well, they were all in pieces back at the main cabin. It would take some poor bastard forever to figure out whose arm was whose, whose leg had been shoved up the fat kid's ass, whose head was floating in the toilet, whose penis was floating in the kettle.

They were all gone.

She was the final girl.

And the pig-faced maniac was closing the gap on her.

She tripped, for the umpteenth time, and followed it up with an involuntary cartwheel. Landing on her backside with enough force to rattle her teeth, she thought, *Why can't I stay on my feet?* She had always been quite good at walking – she'd done it since she was a kid – and running was just walking but at a quicker pace, was it not? And yet here she was, struggling like some one-year-old amateur wearing oversized jelly-sandals.

Then, he appeared from behind a tree, the pig-masked maniac, swinging his axe the from side to side, taking the tops off nettle- and raspberry-bushes as if they'd done something to offend him. *"Squeeee!"* he said. The girl didn't know what that meant, but she had a feeling he wasn't offering her a truce or apologising for butchering her friends – and twelve others that would, if this were a movie – remain uncredited.

"Fuck you!" she screamed, clambering to her feet with the faux optimism that she would stay there. "Fuck you, you pig-faced fuck!" Her mother would have reproached her for using such foul language had she been present, but the girl was in shock, and it was a known fact that shocked people liked to say *fuck* a lot.

"Squeeeeeeee!" Pigface said, reached behind his back. When his hand reappeared it was clenching Billy's decapitated head, which was swinging to and fro by its hair. Billy stared out at her, almost accusatory.

What did I do? she thought. *It wasn't my fault your head was so loose. It wasn't my fault you got in the way of his axe-blade. Quit looking at me like that you...*

"Reeeeeee!" the killer said, kicking the head away. It didn't get far. In fact, it came back to him by way of a tree, but that was the thing about woods. You couldn't move for all the goddamn trees.

The girl turned and ran once again. She had a stitch in her side, and her bare feet were battered and bloody, but she still had a head, and while she had a head, she had a chance...

As the girl crested the hill, she saw a cabin. Her heart sank as she realised she'd completed a full circle and was back at Camp Diamond Creek. How was that even *possible*? Had she not been running in a straight line? Was one leg marginally shorter than the other? Whatever it was, the girl could have cried as she went ass over tit down the hill, rolling toward the familiar cabin at a speed that gained her a few hundred metres on Mr Bacon, who was *squee*-ing and *reeee*-ing behind her like some weird human siren. She hit the side of the cabin, and would have gone all the way through it had it not been constructed from only the finest logs. It hurt, but she could walk – at least, she could walk in pretty much the same way a drunken geriatric could walk – and she wasted no time in getting to her feet and rushing around the side of the cabin.

"Squeeee!"

It sounded far away, but the woods had a way of distorting things – like rotating when people are walking in a straight line just to fuck with their minds. She could trust the woods no more than she could trust the porcine psycho pursuing her.

"You didn't bring him *back*?" a voice whispered. The final girl almost shat her knickers. She snapped her head to the left and found another girl staring back at her, all wide eyes and fearfulness. Obviously one of the counsellors, she wore the yellow and black uniform and a sticker with her camp name on it: *Moose*. Quite apt it was, too. "You *did*, didn't you? You brought him back to the fucking camp?"

The girl shrugged. "I didn't mean to," she whispered. "I was running, and I kept falling over, and I must have got disorientated, and I don't know why I'm trying to explain myself to you, Moose, not when he's still out there." Then, something hit the girl, something terrible, and it was all she could do not to scream.

She *wasn't* the final girl. There was a fifty-percent chance *Moose* was the final girl, the one destined to survive long enough to relay the previous night's horrific events to the police. Those weren't great odds.

"Who *is* he? What does he want from us? Why is he wearing a pig mask?" All reasonable questions, the girl thought.

Moose pushed herself up against the cabin and took a quick peek. "I don't know," she said. "And I don't know what he wants from us. All I know is that he's really fucking angry. He killed the other counsellors, which is a bit of a pain in the ass as I really liked one of them." She stared skyward, as if recollecting a pleasant moment, or one that might have been had pig-face not hacked everyone to death. The half-smile disappeared from her face. "You can't be here. *I'm* the final girl. There can't be two final girls. You're just going to have to carry on running through the trees until he finds you."

The hell I will, the girl thought. "What makes *you* so special?" she said. "The counsellors never survive. You might as well just lie down and wait for him to get you.”

“I’m not just a counsellor!” Moose said, and then lowered her voice to add, “I’m also a virgin. Everyone knows that the virgins don’t die. How many miles of cock have you had?”

The girl shook her head. “None of your damn business,” she said. “But being a virgin doesn’t guarantee you safety. One of the guys I was camping with, Roger, he was bug-ugly even *before* he went through the wood-chipper. There’s no way he *wasn’t* a virgin, and yet Pigface got him.”

“Hookers,” Moose said. “Your friend Roger must have been paying for it. If he’d laid off on the crack-whores, he’d still be alive now.”

The girl considered Moose’s theory for a moment, and quickly dismissed it as bullshit. “Why don’t we just split up?” she said. “That way, Pigface will get whoever he gets, and the other will live to tell the tale.”

Moose was about to speak when an axe appeared behind her. Attached to the axe was the porcine maniac. Before Moose had time to open her mouth, the axe came down, splitting her head in two like a chunk of firewood. Blood sprayed out at the girl – the *final* girl – and she backed away, wiping it from her eyes. For a moment, everything was blurry and bloody. It was like looking through a pink lava lamp. Still, she could make out Moose's split face, the way the nose lopsidedly dangled to the left, the way one of her eyes had popped from its socket and now hung there like a busted yoyo.

"Squeeee!" Pigface said, yanking the axe from Moose's not-quite-evenly divided head. There was a crunch, which reminded the final girl of her younger brother at breakfast-time. Noisy little bastard chomped like a starving camel.

Moose the Unfortunate Counsellor dropped to her knees, her head and face hanging down like a half-peeled banana.

Blood pumped from lord knows where, peppering the ground around the final girl's feet. For some reason, it made her need the toilet. Now, however, was not the time. It was time to run, to run away from Pigface. She didn't know if he was aware of the 'final girl' rule. Out there in the middle of nowhere, there was a good chance he hadn't heard of Speak and Spell or russet flares, either.

She turned and ran as fast as she could, which wasn't that fast, but Pigface didn't seem to be in any rush to go after her. Maybe he had heard of the 'final girl' rule after all.

Reaching the cabin she'd spent the last week in, she searched for something – *anything* – to protect herself with. It was just after midnight, and all of the trucks and cars parked up on the gravel at the front of the main cabin, including the VW camper she and her friends had travelled to Camp Diamond Creek in, had fallen prey to a pair of garden shears. Wires and tubes hung from their hoods as if they had been disembowelled.

The girl was trapped, her chance of escape about as realistic as Christopher Reeves' flying scenes in a film she'd caught at the pictures the previous week. And so it made perfect sense to equip herself as best she could.

Rifling through the drawers, pushing aside Deborah and Kaycee's marvellous collection of dildos and grimacing as she did so, she found a box of matches and a small Swiss Army knife that might have answered the question about why the Swiss weren't terribly good in wars.

It was better than nothing – *just* – and though it would hardly put the fear of day into Pigface, she felt vaguely better armed than she had been unarmed.

Slipping out into the night, the girl edged around her cabin. From where she stood, she could make out the big cabin on top of the hill – often a place of joy, of Kumbayah and handclapping, of woodwork classes and foraging expeditions, and now...well now it was a morgue, only warm and full of flies. She didn't want to go up there, but she knew that's where it would all end.

The big finale.

You couldn't hope to defeat an axe-wielding maniac without a big finale. She could run around in the woods all night long, and he would be there, just a few feet behind. If she *was* the final girl (she was taking nothing for granted, not since the Moose episode) they could be at it until winter broke, or until she starved to death, whichever came first.

No, she had to go up to the main cabin, to where the decimated bodies of her friends lay around like Jeffrey Dahmer's scatter-cushions. It was Pigface's hub, the place she knew he would return to once he was bored of searching for her. It was best to get up there and catch him unaware. Maybe set some traps, or whatever traps were possible from a box of – she opened the matchbox – *two* matches and a knife that was primarily made up of toothpicks, nail-files, and screwdrivers.

The thought sent a shiver along her spine. *Go with your friends*, her mother had said just last week. *Go, have fun, it's your last chance before college.*

Thanks, Mom. I'm having a fucking blast, you old bat.

The girl opened the knife out onto a particularly savage looking pair of toenail clippers and headed up the hill, listening out for any twig-crunches that weren't her own. Pigface wasn't behind her, or in front of her, or at either side of her, which was great news as far as she was concerned, but then she thought, *What if he's underneath me, or swinging through the trees like some swinish Tarzan?* If nothing else, it made her walk a little faster.

As she neared the main cabin, she heard music drifting along on the breeze. Bob Dylan was babbling on about how the answer to various questions was blowing in the wind. It transpired that the wind was, in fact, a bothersome know-it-all.

Someone must have left a record on the player. Or maybe Pigface had decided a little music was what the night needed, something to break up the constant, awkward silences that passed between predator and victim – when he wasn't *squee*-ing and she wasn't squealing.

Upon reaching the door, the girl took a deep breath. The music was louder now, which tended to happen the closer you got to something. The song finished, and then there was an almighty scratch before it started over from the beginning.

Someone was in the cabin already.

Pigface?

She glanced down at the toenail-clippers in her hand. He had an axe. It didn't seem fair. Like pitting a tiger against a shih-tzu. Didn't final girls usually get a kitchen knife, or a set of knitting needles, or the killer's accidentally misplaced machete? It didn't bode well for her survival.

She stepped into the main cabin and slowly made her way past the acoustic guitars lining the hall. That was when the stench hit the back of her throat. God, it was pungent. The dead kids were starting to pong. Worse than when they were alive. The only thing 'blowing in the wind' in that moment was the stench of a dozen slowly-rotting hippies.

The girl managed to swallow back the vomit and, stepping over what looked like two arms holding hands, made her way into the assembly hall.

It was worse than she remembered, though she had previously only caught a glimpse of it. I don't care who you are, the sight of a blood-drenched, axe-brandishing maniac in a pig mask has the tendency to set your feet a-running. And run she had, and trip over repeatedly she had, and whimper, well that wasn't something you could control when you were running and tripping over...

There seemed to be a lot more bodies in the hall now...or a lot more pieces of the *same* bodies. Yes, that was it. Arms and legs had been quartered. Heads had been split. Genitals had been de-sacked and rolled along the floorboards like some sick game of bloody marbles.

"Gurgh," the girl said. It wasn't a word – except in Haiti, where it meant 'fish bollocks'. Luckily, one of the attachments of the Swiss Army knife was a little vial of smelling-salts. She felt better once she'd had a couple of snorts.

The Bob Dylan song stopped, and this time it stayed stopped. The girl didn't like the silence, which was ridiculous since she was standing in a roomful of hewn teenagers. Silence was the last thing that should have unnerved her.

"Squeeeee!" Pigface said, stepping from behind the brightly-painted backdrop she and her friends were going to use in their amateur performance of *The Wizard of Oz*. His axe dripped with viscera, his white apron was...well, not *white* at all. He looked even more maniacal than ever standing in front of the Emerald City.

She held both hands out and took a deep breath. "Have you not heard about the final girl decree?" she said. It was worth a shot.

"The final girl *what*?" Pigface said, lowering his axe for the time being. It was the first time she'd heard him speak. He had a soft voice, which she hadn't been anticipating at all. It was the kind of voice one might expect from a pilot just before he broke all laws of physics and carted three-hundred people toward the heavens.

"It's how this *works*," the girl said. "Everyone knows about it."

"Well *I* don't," he said, his words slightly muffled by the mask. "Why does no-one tell me anything. When did this start?"

The girl scratched her head. "Only this last year or so. Shit, you're having a bad day, aren't you?"

Pigface snorted. "Story of my life," he said. "So you're the final girl then, are you?"

"Since you killed all the others except for me," she said, gesturing to the bits and bobs that were obviously female scattered across the floor, "I guess I am."

"Well that's a nuisance," he said, shrinking. He was clearly annoyed at this new information. "I've been chasing you all night long. I'll bet you were wondering what the hell was going on, weren't you." He sniggered and leaned the axe against the theatrical backdrop. It now looked as if one of the munchkins was giving the handle a BJ.

"I did think it was a *little* odd," the girl said, smiling. "I mean, if I'd've known you didn't know about the final girl decree, I'd have hollered back over my shoulder. Saved us both a bit of energy."

"Did you have a stitch, too?" Pigface said. The girl nodded. "I swear, I thought I was going to cough up a lung. For a little thing, you're pretty spritely."

"Thanks," she said. "You're no dawdler yourself."

"I have good days and bad," he said, sucking in his stomach. "So what happens now? I mean, you say I can't kill you, and I've killed everything else, so I guess that's it. Time to call it a night."

"Yeah, I think we'll both sleep tonight," she said. "Good job you got that Moose girl first."

"Oh, yeah! Did you see the way her head split?"

"I *did*!" the girl said. "I'm wearing most of it."

"Sorry about that. Sometimes the axe gets away from me. I was thinking about upgrading to something less messy. A nice clean scythe, perhaps. Or one of those things they use to slice cheese."

"No, your axe does a good job," the girl said, turning the Swiss Army knife over in her hand so that the toenail clippers faced forwards. "That's kind of your thing now."

"Yeah, I suppose," Pigface said, though he didn't sound convinced. He took a few steps toward the girl, leaving his axe behind. "Well, I guess you'd better clear off, then," he said. "Be sure to tell your friends about the infamous Camp Diamond Creek killer."

"Oh, I will," the girl said, taking a step toward Pigface. They were almost close enough to kiss now. The girl could smell his breath as it seeped through the tiny slit-hole in his mask. She was pretty sure he'd had curry for supper. "I'll tell everyone how I avenged the deaths of my friends, and twelve nonentities, by stabbing the great Camp Diamond Creek killer in the side of the head with a pair of blunt toenail-clippers."

"Huh?"

She brought the Swiss Army knife up and slammed it into Pigface's temple. He *squeeeeeeeeed!* as he went down. As a weapon, the girl's was practically useless, but it had caught him so unexpectedly that it gave her just enough time to lunge across the room, to where the axe leant against the yellow brick road.

Snatching it up, she spun around just in time to watch Pigface disappear through a door at the rear of the cabin. Apparently, he didn't like the taste of his own medicine; nor did he fancy having his head lopped off.

The girl rushed across the room, almost slipping on three-of-twelve's giblets. She reached the door a little more quickly thanks to the thick coating of blood and grey matter on her bare soles. She knew exactly what lay beyond the door, which was why she was in no rush to hack it down with Pigface's axe.

"You do know you've shut yourself in the toilet?" the girl said, tapping at the door with the axe-blade.

"Erm," Pigface said. "Where's the light-switch?"

"Face the door and it's to your left." The girl felt terribly guilty all of a sudden, but the bastard *had* killed sixteen kids in the most brutal of ways. "Found it?"

There was an audible *dink!* from the other side of the door. "Yeah. I appear to have locked myself in the toilet. Don't suppose you want to let me out and give me a head start, do you, only I've got to be home for sunrise, otherwise my mom will start to worry."

The girl couldn't believe what she was hearing. "What about the parents of the kids you've slaughtered? How do you think they're going to feel when they find out their beloved offspring have been massacred? Do you have any idea how important some of those kids were? Roger, the guy you fed into the chipper, he was working on a cure for cancer. He almost had it, too. Another few weeks' work, he reckoned. And Kaycee was going to be the world's first lesbian lumberjack. She had a name for her business, and everything, but you ruined that. Now there will never be a *Faux-fellas Tree-fellers*. You ought to be ashamed of yourself you sick sonofabitch, but I don't think you are, *are* you?"

Silence, and then what sounded like a petrified fart.

"No, I don't think you're ever coming out of that toilet," the girl said, removing the matchbox from her hot-pants pocket. She didn't want to move too far from the door, lest Pigface realise she wasn't there and seize the opportunity to escape, but she needed something flammable.

In the staff kitchen area she found a half-full bottle of *Crisco*, and since that stuff was more combustible than Ozzy Osbourne's liquor-cabinet, she carried it out to the main hall, to where the toilet door remained engaged.

As she began to pour and slosh the cooking oil up the door, her conscience returned. *What are you doing? You're not a killer. At least use something that isn't going to make the place smell like fries for miles around.*

"What's that smell?" Pigface said, nervously. "Is that...is that cooking oil?"

"I can't find any gasoline," the girl said. "Don't suppose you know where there is any?"

Pigface sighed. "If you go out through the front door, take a right, you'll see a little hut about...wait a minute, are you going to set fire to me?"

"Well, you're hardly going to set fire to *yourself*, are you?" the girl said, taking a step away from the oil pooling around her feet.

"I'd rather you *didn't*," Pigface said. "What if I hand myself in? What if I pop off home and get my mom to call the police first thing in the morning? I'm sure there will be a reward. I've been doing this for years, and the local Sheriff's department will be chuffed to bits once I'm behind bars."

"You've been doing this for *years*?" the girl asked, incredulous. "Why isn't there a warning or something as you enter the camp?"

"I took it down," Pigface said. "Puts people off. No, all-in-all I've probably killed a hundred teens, all of them up to no good, on drugs or having orgies. There's a picture of me up in the Sheriff's office, but it's just a rudimentary sketch of a pig. Probably why I haven't been caught."

"Until *now*," the girl reminded him. "Tonight, your reign of terror ends. Tonight, this final girl is going to finish you once and for all. You're not supernatural or anything, are you? I mean, you're not liable to come back to life if I set you on fire?"

"Doubt it," Pigface said. "Immortality doesn't run in my family."

That was good news. The last thing the final girl wanted was to kill Pigface now, only to hear of his return on this exact date a year from now, or whenever a new group of kids decided on a camping trip. That would be *awful*.

"Do you have any last words?" the girl asked. It seemed only fair.

"*Shit* seems appropriate," Pigface said.

The final girl removed one match from the box and struck it. Of course, it went out. Sod's law. She dropped it, cursed once or twice, and took out the second – and final – match.

"Everything okay out there?" Pigface said. "Having a change of heart?" He sounded optimistic.

"Not on your nelly, bacon-face!" She struck the match, and this time it worked. She took a tentative step back before dropping it. Good job she did, because the door went up like the apartment block in that film with Steve McQueen and Paul Newman.

"Aaaargh!" Pigface screeched. "It's a bit warm in here!"

The final girl didn't stick around to hear the murderous bastard die. She picked up the axe and ran, and ran, and ran, and she didn't stop until she reached the road running around Diamond Creek.

Back in the main cabin the fiery door flew open, and a charred shape emerged. It threw itself down and rolled around for a minute or two. Satisfied that the flames were extinguished, the burnt and blackened figure sat up and stared around in utter confusion. "Hello?" he said, though his voice cracked. A singed windpipe will do that to a person. "Have you gone?" He sighed, put the final girl's atrocious act before skedaddling down to hormones, and climbed to his feet. "That's it," he said, dusting flakes of burnt skin from his person. "I quit."

2

An Old Dusty Road – 2014

The beige-and-white camper rolled along the road, leaving a miasma of dirt and dust in its wake. It was the kind of vehicle that one wouldn't trust with a quick trip to the shops at the bottom of the street. And yet people filled them with bodies and dragged them thousands of miles across the country, tempting fate and hitting squirrels and skunks as if they had a personal vendetta against nature. It was the kind of vehicle that had no original parts, so in essence it was an entirely different camper to when it was first purchased. It was the kind of vehicle that only assholes and hippies drove.

"I-Spy with my little eye..." its driver, Bailey Painter, said, absorbing their surroundings, looking for anything other than dust and sunshine. "Something beginning with...D."

"Dust," Melissa Voorhees said with a heavy sigh. You see, Bailey Painter wasn't the sharpest tool in the drawer. In fact, he wasn't as sharp *as* the drawer. He was what most people would call simple, and that worked just fine for him. He was good at sports, and as far as he was concerned, that was better than learning *words*, and *things*, and *stuff* that he would never use once he left college. To him, pi was something you ate, trigonometry was the art of shooting, and bosons were those big hairy bastards that liked to stampede.

"I-Spy with my little eye..." Bailey started, but the others had had enough, and let him know by way of a collective groan.

"Can we just listen to the radio?" Lakresha Loomis said. "We've been playing I-Spy for eight hours, and I don't know about y'all, but I'm done."

"She's right," Junior Kramer said, taking his girlfriend's hand. "I know we said no radio, but I think now's the time to break that rule." *Before we all go mental*, he thought but didn't add.

"Look!" Freddy Crowley said, poking at a window with an excited finger. "Only twenty miles to Diamond Creek."

All seven of them whooped and hollered. It had been a long journey, and they were all at breaking point. You could be the best of friends at the start of a long journey, but by the time you arrived, three of your party wouldn't be talking, two others had filed for divorce, and someone had decided suicide was a much better premise and jumped from the van a few miles back. The heat didn't help matters. It was hotter than Georgia asphalt outside, and marginally cooler than Hell inside.

"It's about time," Amanda Bateman said, tucking sweaty strands of hair behind her ears. "I swear, if I don't get water soon, I'm going to pass out." Amanda was beautiful. At least, *Freddy* thought she was. She was the kind of girl he'd be glad to take home to his momma. Long blonde hair, freckles running across the bridge of her nose, cute dimples when she smiled; she was everything he looked for in a girl, and she didn't even know it.

"We're going to have to stop before we reach the camp anyway," Bailey said across his shoulder. Only Melissa sat up front with him, which left five of them cramped into the back.

"Why stop now?" Cedric Myers, the token-geek, said. "We're almost there."

Melissa glanced down at the fuel gauge, saw the needle dipping in and out of the red, and said, "Because *genius* here has driven past three gas stations, and now we're running on fumes."

"What?"

"Fuck, dude!"

"Shit, Bailey, were you dropped on your head as a child?"

"Do you even gas, brah?"

Bailey squirmed in his sweat-pooled seat. "I didn't know what that little needle meant until just," he said. "I thought it measured the distances between gas stations."

"Fuck, are we going to break down out here?" Amanda said. She knew a thing or two about survival, so long as there was something to survive on. On all four sides of the camper was sand and dust. Even Bear Grylls would have struggled to cobble together a decent meal.

Lakresha released Junior's hand and all but stood up in the back of the camper. Clicking her fingers as she spoke, she said, "Y'all out of your damn minds if you think I'm walking anywhere in these heels. And I ain't sitting in no portable oven, waiting on your dumb ass to come back with gas." She was specifically targeting Bailey with her rant, but if there was anyone they wouldn't trust to fetch more fuel, it was him. He'd come back with a six-pack of brewskies, an extra-large bag of Cheetos, a vacant expression, and nothing else.

"I knew something like this was going to happen," Cedric said, writing something down in his notebook. He had one of those pens with the annoying toppers. His was a miniature Captain Kirk figure. Cedric was a huge Trekkie, and very much a virgin. He'd once kissed his second cousin twice removed, but that didn't really count since they were both drunk at the time (one beer, one cider) and he'd subsequently forgotten all about it.

"Why do you have to write everything down in that dumb book of yours?" Junior said, snatching it up from the table.

"Hey! Give that back," he said, with about as much conviction as an agoraphobic traveller.

"Ladonna was the feisty one?" Junior said, reading from the book. "She was hot, but not as hot as Anna. Anna was the kind of girl I'd like to shoot my—"

Cedric snatched the book out of Junior's hands. "Do you mind? That's *private*." He slammed it shut and tucked it away in his backpack. They would never know what he wanted to shoot, now. Talk about a cliffhanger.

"That's your novel, is it?" Junior said, only mildly irritated. Cedric was no threat to him, or anyone else for that matter. He was just an annoying geek, only dangerous in chess club. "You're writing about us but changing the names..."

"That's not *true*," Cedric said, feigning shock.

"So Ladonna is nothing to do with Lakresha? And Anna, the kind of girl you would like to shoot your god knows what over her *lordy* knows what, isn't, in fact, Amanda?"

"Ew," Amanda said. "No offence, Cedric."

"None taken," Cedric said. "And no. Those are completely made up names for completely made up people. Do you have any idea how fiction works?"

"Do you have any idea how this *fist* works?" Junior said, clenching his right hand as tightly as possible.

"Guys, guys, guys!" Freddy said, climbing to his feet. "There's no need for this. Cedric's novel has nothing to do with us, and Amanda is safe from whatever gun Cedric's thinking of shooting, so why don't we all just take a chill pill and concentrate on the problem at hand." He was of course referring to the fact that they were about to judder to an unexpected stop. Campers don't run on fumes for long, especially not ones packed to the roof-rack with teenagers.

"Panic over," Bailey said, slamming the steering-wheel with unreserved joy. "I knew there'd be another stop before Diamond Creek." He spun the wheel a full rotation, pulling the camper onto what sounded like a gravel track and felt like a sea of child-skulls. When Bailey saw the bearded maniac sitting on a broken bench in front of the gas station – dungarees, chewing tobacco, a lot of hair, none of it one his head – he realised the child-skull thing wasn't too far-fetched.

"This isn't a gas station," Lakresha said, glancing out through the side window. "This is where cars and people come to die."

"We need gas, don't we?" Melissa said, nuzzling Bailey's neck and causing him to almost run over some sort of wild dog. Perhaps it was Grizzly Adams's girlfriend. He sure did look the type.

"We need *gas*," Junior said. "Not stabbing and cooking on some hillbilly barbecue."

"Let's not judge this walking cliché until we talk to him," Amanda said. "For all we know, he's just retired. He could have been a doctor, or an engineer, or a—"

"Fucking *prisoner*," Lakresha said. "I ain't setting foot outside of this camper. If you didn't notice, I'm a little bit black. We don't fare well in these situations."

"Oh, come on," Freddy said. "This isn't some dumb horror movie. If it were, we'd have broken down back in the woods, or one of us would have had some incredibly-detailed and brutal vision that we were all going to die, only for death to catch up with us all the same. Since none of us have brought a video camera, it's safe to say that we're not taking part in some low-rent, tedious, by-the-numbers found-footage flick."

"Which leaves us with a hillbilly hacking," Junior said. "I'm staying right here with my woman. If y'all aren't back in five minutes, don't be surprised to find the camper, and us, gone."

Bailey pulled the van alongside the station's only pump. According to the readout, the last person to use it had filled up with a buck-fifty. Goddamn recession – leaving people out in the sticks since 2009.

"Okay," Bailey said, shutting the engine off. "In and out, people. I'll get the gas. How does it work again?"

"I'll help, honey" Melissa said. She was slightly smarter than Bailey, and there was a collective sigh of relief when she offered her services. Bailey would have tried to shove the pump nozzle up the exhaust. "Can someone get me something to drink?"

"Me too!" Lakresha said. "But if it looks like blood, and smells like blood, there's a good chance it *is* blood. Make sure the seal isn't broken. And whatever you do, don't accept anything he has to offer food-wise. They eat some crazy shit out here, like roadkill, and jellied eels, and recently-deceased family members."

Freddy pushed open the side doors and stepped down onto the gravel. Stretching and yawning, he turned to Amanda. "You coming?"

She stood and carefully lowered herself down from the camper, completely ignoring Freddy's offered hand. "I could drink a pint of piss out of Bigfoot's wellington boot," she said, slapping her lips together. "Of course I'm coming."

Freddy managed to supress his smile.

"Do you think he has a toilet?" Cedric said, climbing out of the van and glancing around for anything that looked remotely...*toilet*-y.

"I'd be surprised if he could tell you the difference between a toilet and his living room," Junior said, settling Lakresha onto his knee. "But look around, dude. Even if he *does* have a toilet, is that the kind of place you want to use?"

"That's a universal misconception," Cedric said, pushing his glasses up onto the bridge of his nose, popping a zit or two on the way. "The toilet seat is not a common vehicle for transmitting infections and

STDs to humans, unless you're rubbing your genitals all over the place or licking the ceramics, which I won't be."

"Rather you than me," Lakresha said. "I'd rather shake my lettuce in a beehive, if you know what I mean."

"Now that," Cedric said, "*would* be dangerous."

"Come on," Amanda said. "Let's get this over with, before Duck Dynasty over there gets a chance to call his brothers for back-up."

They made their way toward the store, where the bearded man had started to play a harmonica...badly. When he saw them approaching, he wiped the harmonica on the front of his dungarees and slipped it into his breast pocket. Toothless grins are cute on babies, but on geriatric gas-station attendants, they're creepy as hell.

"Excuse me, sir," Freddy said, coming to a stop in front of the proprietor. "We ran out of gas. We're looking to fill up and get some drinks for the road." He smiled a mouthful of gleaming white teeth, but it almost felt like bragging, and so slapped his mouth shut as quickly as he'd opened it.

The hillbilly, or "Ozzie" according to the name sewn onto his dungarees, whistled, though it was probably unintentional given his lack of choppers. "We got gas," he said. "Lots of the stuff, if you got the green."

Freddy, Amanda, and Cedric exchanged glances. What did he think they were going to pay with? Blowjobs and compliments?

"We've got money," Amanda said, reaching into her purse. Freddy clandestinely tapped her on the shoulder and shook his head: *don't get your wallet out here...*

"Now that's not very nice," Ozzie said, pushing himself up from the bench. Several of his bones cracked in unison and, three miles away, a flock of birds flew from a telegraph pole. He started walking toward the store. "This here is a family business. My pa owned it before me, and his pa before him. We is good, honest people that don't appreciate being judged just 'cause we look like we could have crawled out of a Louisiana swamp."

The trio began to follow Ozzie. It wasn't difficult; he had all the speed of an apprehensive sloth. With each step he took, something creaked, suggesting he was slightly older than World War II and marginally younger than the Pine Ridge Campaign. Either he had a terrible limp, or there was a chunk of gravel in his boot.

"He didn't mean anything by it," Cedric said. "We're just not used to being out of the 'burbs."

"That's the thing about you city-types," Ozzie said, leading the way into the store, which comprised of ten badly-stocked shelves and a small, buzzing refrigerator. Unless Ozzie was a mass-murderer of imps, gnomes, faeries, or gremlins, there were no bodies contained within. "Y'all come out here, *judging*. Judging and *mocking*. So what we don't brush our beards, and every now and then one of us marries a goat. Y'all have no right to come out here and stare and point at us like the world's some giant damn fishbowl."

"I'm sorry," Freddy said, holding his hand palm out, placatory. "Won't happen again, sir."

Ozzie stared vacantly at the extended hand for a moment, and then said, "Now, we don't have much in the way of drinks." He began rifling through a series of unopened boxes stacked against the wall. "Got some beetroot juice, if that's any good for ya. Oh, and I just had a delivery of vinegar, 'bout three months ago. If you only have a few mouthfuls, you should be okay. Friend of mine, god rest his soul, died after one glass of the stuff, but he had a dodgy ticker. Do any of you suffer from heart disease?"

Amanda didn't realise she was scrunching her face up until she went to scratch her nose and found her bottom lip there. "We'll pass on the vinegar," she said. "What about water?"

Ozzie shook his head. "Ain't no call for water around these parts," he said. "Friend of mine, god rest his soul, once drank a glass of the stuff, but he had typhoid, and..."

Outside, a horn honked. When they looked out through the front window, Bailey was holding up the bone-dry nozzle.

"Your friend's an impatient little prick, ain't he?" Ozzie said, making his way across the room to a small, red button next to the register. He pushed it. Fuel began to spurt from the end of the nozzle, and Bailey panicked, spinning around, coating everything within two metres in premium unleaded. Melissa snatched the nozzle from her boyfriend and the gas ceased geysering. She hadn't told him about how the trigger worked.

"Do you have a toilet I could use?" Cedric asked. He'd been hopping from foot to foot for an entire minute, working up the courage to speak. An escaped trickle told him that time was of the essence.

"Got a *hole*," Ozzie said. "No paper, though, if it's a number two you want to do."

"And where can I find this hole?" Cedric said. He'd gone a strange colour; almost mauve.

"Through the back," Ozzie said. "You can't miss it. I left a little something in there this morning."

Great, Cedric thought. "That little something wouldn't happen to be an air-freshener, would it?" *No, of course it wouldn't.*

"We don't sell air fresheners," Ozzie said. "Friend of mine once ate one, but he had a...*hey*, don't you want to hear what happened to Buzz?"

Cedric had already vanished through the door at the back of the store.

"Be careful!" Ozzie called after him. "I've fallen in once or twice. It's a lot deeper than it looks." He turned his attention back to Freddy and Amanda. "Now, what can I get you fine folks? Have you heard the new

Johnny Cash album?" He held up a cassette copy of *Unchained*, an album released in 1996, though neither Freddy nor Amanda knew that. All they knew was that if Johnny Cash *did* release a new album, it would be something of a miracle.

"Don't suppose you have the new one from The Carpenters?" Freddy said. Amanda nudged him hard in the side. He thought it was funny, even if she didn't.

Ozzie shook his head. "All I've got is Johnny Cash." He placed the cassette back down onto the counter and sighed. "So what are you kids doing out here?" *Other than harassing me and turning down the man in black*, he thought but didn't say.

"We're heading up to Camp Diamond Creek for the week," Freddy said. "Sort of a mini-break before we go back to college."

Past Ozzie's beard and the remnants of mouldy food it harboured, his mouth had fallen wide open. It was like staring into some Lovecraftian abyss; Freddy was waiting for a tentacle to pop out.

"Is he okay?" Amanda whispered into Freddy's ear.

"I think he's had a stroke or something," Freddy said, leaning across and staring into the old hillbilly's terrified eyes. "Do you want us to call an ambulance?" he said, as loudly as possible. "It might take a few hours to get here, but that's better than nothing."

"Did you dumbasses say you were going up to Camp Diamond Creek?" Ozzie said. Amanda heaved a sigh of relief. The thought of administering mouth-to-mouth sickened her to the stomach.

"Ah, you're back with us," Freddy said. "That's right. We're up there for a week. Foraging, campfires, occasional recreational drug use, you know the drill." He didn't know whether any of the others had brought drugs – other than ibuprofen and Robitussin – but if he knew Melissa and Bailey as well as he *thought* he did, they'd have a little something aromatic stashed away for the cold nights.

"You *can't* go up there!" Ozzie said, almost shouted. He grabbed Freddy by the arms and began to shake him as if trying to dislodge a tricky shit. "You must stay away from Camp Diamond Creek! D'ya *hear* me? Stay *away*!"

Freddy shook the mad old bastard off. For a skinny fella, he had some strength. Like Sigourney Weaver. "What's the matter with you, man?" he said, rubbing at his arms. "Jeez, You almost cut me with your calluses!"

Ozzie backed away, as if he suddenly realised he was talking to vampires. "Heed my words," he said, pushing the button which cut off the fuel supply. "That place is doomed! *Doomed*, I tell you!"

"That's all very melodramatic," Amanda said, frowning just enough to stuff a deck of playing cards in her forehead.

"Thanks," Ozzie said, smiling coyly. "Three years at Juilliard." He became serious once again, his mouth in a wide O, his eyes wide enough for them to fall out and roll along the dirty gas-station floor. "Doomed, I tell you!"

"What's doomed?" Cedric said, walking across the store and zipping himself up. He looked rather pleased for a man who'd just pissed into a hole.

"Doesn't matter," Freddy said. To Ozzie, he said, "How much do we owe you for the gas?"

"Twenty-five dollars," Ozzie said, ringing it up on the register. "Would have been less but your friend put three litres on my forecourt."

Amanda paid the man and turned to leave.

"DOOOOOOMED!" Ozzie said once again. When they were out of the store, talking amongst themselves, he smiled. "Nice kids. Hope they take the hint and head on home."

"OZZIE!" a shrill, female voice called from somewhere out back.

"Yes, dear?" Ozzie said with a heavy sigh.

"Your barbecue penis is ready!"

"Thanks, dear. I'll be there in a minute."

He watched as the camper van pulled away, back onto the road, back on its way to Camp Diamond Creek, which was, if you haven't been paying attention, pretty.

3
Camp Diamond Creek – 2014

The trees stretched up on either side of the van as they approached. Off in the distance, a whippoorwill chirruped cheerily. At least, that's what it sounded like to the teens in the camper. If you were to run it through some sort of whippoorwill-to-human translation machine, though, you would have heard, "Doomed! You're all dooooooooomed!" Still, such things were yet to be invented, and even if they had, a group of hormonal vacationists wouldn't have had the gumption or the capital to buy one.

"Finally," Lakresha said, jabbing a perfectly-manicured finger toward the battered and bullet-pocked sign at the edge of the road. CAMP DIAMOND CREEK – WHERE DREAMS CAN COME TRUE IF YOU WANT THEM TO.

Bailey steered the camper up a steep incline. There was nothing either side of them, unless you considered empty space and certain death as *something*. Suddenly, everyone in the van wished they were driving, and not the guy who had doused himself, his girlfriend, the van, and Ozzie's forecourt in gas a few miles back.

"It's beautiful!" Amanda said, gazing dreamily out through the dust-flecked window. She liked trees, and shrubs, and things that lived on trees and shrubs. She was what certain people referred to as a 'tree-hugger'. She was the main reason Freddy Crowley wished he was a tree.

"Doesn't look to be any tracks," Melissa said, leaning forwards in the passenger seat. "I don't think there are going to be many people up here."

"Good!" Junior said. "More for my baby and me." He tugged on Lakresha's jeans, pulling her in for a quick fondle. The swift slap across the bridge of his nose stopped him in his tracks. "Chill, baby," he said. "This is meant to be an enjoyable experience. Remember?"

"I'll remember that if you remember to keep your hands to yourself unless otherwise instructed." She sat at the table across from Cedric and started applying make-up, as if they were about to embark upon a week at Whore School and not seven days in the wilderness.

As the camper crested the hill, the trees opened out to reveal a car-park. There was only one other vehicle – a van with the camp's logo printed on its side. Bailey pulled the camper up next to it and switched off the engine.

"Quieter than I thought it would be," Freddy said, collecting his luggage from the cupboard/ironing-board-storage-unit/shoe-room.

"On the bright side," Amanda said, sliding open the side-door, "the communal showering isn't going to be so freaky."

Freddy almost fell into the cupboard. *Communal showering? As in together? Naked? Wet and naked? Together, wet and naked?* He must have missed that part in the brochure; it was far too late for a penis enlargement. *Maybe,* he thought, *I can fashion something out of bacon.* If he had any chance of getting together with Amanda, he'd have to use his wits. Yes, bacon, and perhaps some sort of haggis...

They all gathered their belongings and left the camper – Melissa and Lakresha were the last to exit the vehicle, since they had apparently decided the best way to camp was to pack everything they owned

"Planning on staying for good?" Cedric said, gesturing to the pile of precariously-stacked suitcases.

"Up yours, geek," Melissa said. "Just because all you brought was a Gameboy and a fanny-pack filled with Warhammer toys."

Cedric flipped her the bird. "It's a Sega Game Gear, actually, and they're not toys. They're figures. Soon-to-be hand-painted Mangler Squigs and Ruglud's Armoured Orcs."

"Do me, now," Lakresha said, before erupting with laughter. Melissa joined in, as did Bailey. Freddy could see they were already getting to Cedric, that it was going to be a long week for the poor sonofabitch unless he stood up for himself. If it came to it, he'd step in, or at least have a quiet word with the culpable trio. Freddy liked Cedric; he was good to have around, especially if you needed something adding up quickly, or if someone asked you to name all forty-four presidents in the order they were inaugurated. It wasn't a question that came up too often — or at all, for that matter —

but when it *did*, they would have Cedric to answer it.

Amanda had slipped away from the group. As the only girl that hadn't packed for six months in the Antarctic, it was relatively easy for her to detach herself. She liked her own space, which was why she'd agreed to come along. Once they were settled, she had plans of her own. She had exploring to do, trees to catalogue, wildlife to observe. Camp Diamond Creek was perfectly situated, miles away from civilisation. You couldn't even hear the traffic from the road they'd just left.

Probably because theirs was the only vehicle to have come this way in hours – maybe days.

Something caught her eye through the trees. A dark shape, moving too quickly for her to catch a proper look at. She squinted, lowered her rucksack to the ground, and edged slowly toward the bushes in front of her. When she could go no further, she pushed aside the shrubbery and stared into the darkness.

That was when the gorilla roared and leapt out at her. She threw herself back, landing on the grass with a thump. Then the ape was all over her. Amanda could feel its fur in her mouth, could smell the sweat as its attack continued.

"Get your paws offa her you damn dirty ape!" a voice said, and then there was a mighty *clunk!* and the gorilla's weight was removed completely. Amanda climbed to her feet to discover Freddy wielding a tin-kettle as if it were the Green Lantern's lamp. The gorilla was rolling around on the floor, saying things like, "Ow," and, "Who hits people with a kettle?!" That was when she realised it wasn't a real gorilla at all, but a fool in a costume. Freddy was about to hit the fucker again when Junior snatched the kettle from his grasp.

"What are you doing, man?" Freddy said, adrenalin coursing through him like never before.

"What are *you* doing?" Junior said, helping the gorilla up. For a gorilla, it was remarkably tame. And also very vocal, and more British than Hugh Grant at a Buckingham Palace garden party. That was when *he* realised it wasn't a gorilla at all, but a British idiot playing dress-up.

"He was trying to molest Amanda!" Freddy said.

"I was trying to *scare* her," the gorilla said, removing its head to reveal a sweaty, freckly, and very ginger boy no older than themselves. There was a slight lump at the top of his forehead from where the spout had made contact. He had more teeth than a Ferrari gearbox, none of which were the same shape or size. "I'm this summer's counsellor. My friend calls me Jay, but you can call me Jason."

"Did you think that was *funny*, Jason?" Lakresha said, stepping toward him, getting into the wide-legged stance that suggested he'd better back down or be prepared to tussle.

"I did when I came up with it," he said, rubbing at his wounded head and hissing through clenched piano-teeth. "It was either this, or I was going to shoot paintballs at you. Guess I should have opted for the paintballs."

Bailey stepped up and wrapped a solid, muscular arm around the counsellor. "Cut my man some slack," he said. "He's just trying to welcome us in the only way he knows how."

"Thank you, good sir," Jason said, nodding his assent.

"Don't *thank* me," Bailey said, pulling the half-dressed gorilla's head down and giving it a damn good noogie. Jason squealed and begged Bailey to stop. "You pull anything like that again, and I'm going to kick your ass so hard, you'll have to part your hair to take a shit."

"Fair enough," Jason said, though it was muffled and high-pitched, and came out sounding more like *furry muff*. Bailey let the beheaded gorilla up for air. "I can see this week's going to be fun." He rubbed at his throat, which was redder than an embarrassed lobster with sunburn.

"Are you okay?" Freddy asked Amanda. She still looked nervous, even though her attacker hadn't really meant her any harm. You see, it's all shits and giggles until someone actually shits.

"I'm fine," she said, forcing a smile. "I just wasn't expecting it." You just didn't go around anticipating an assault from a great ape; if you did, you'd never leave the house.

"Look, I'm really sorry," Jason said. "It's just something we do to set the tone. Most people see the funny side. Trust me, by the end of the week you're going to *love* that kind of shit."

For some reason – perhaps the fur at the back of her throat, or the fact that she was no longer a seven year-old girl – Amanda didn't believe she would.

<h1 style="text-align:center">4</h1>

A Ramshackle Cabin – 2014

The old man threw another bucket of shit into the trees. That made seven, a personal record for Wilbur. If it carried on, he would have to change her diet. There was only so much room in the woods at the back of the cabin. It wouldn't take much for it to start overflowing. *Shit rolls downhill*, or so they say. But if you stacked enough of it, he was pretty sure it would go in any direction it damn well pleased.

"'Twas an evening in October, I'll confess I wasn't sober, I was carting home a load with manly pride," the man sang as he headed back into the sty. "When my feet began to stutter and I fell into the gutter, and a pig came up and lay down by my side." He dropped the bucket into the corner, licking his fingers clean afterwards. He was a dirty sonofabitch, but out there in the middle of nowhere, there was no-one to reproach him, or offer him etiquette lessons, or hook him up with a decent water supply company. The fact that he was old and set in his ways didn't help. You try telling an old person what to do, see where it gets you.

"Then I lay there in the gutter and my heart was all a-flutter, till a lady, passing by, did chance to say: 'You can tell a man that boozes by the company he chooses,' Then the pig got up and slowly walked away."

The man laughed heartily, like a dirty Santa. Drool dripped down his chin, but that was fine. There was a whole mess of silver hair there for such occurrences. His beard was also good for storing food, nesting birds, and tickling Wilbur. "You'd never leave me, would you sweetheart?" he asked the pig, which was sitting in the corner, trying not to make eye-contact. "Old Larry wouldn't last long without you." That was the sorry truth, too. That pig had got him through some tough times. Like the time he'd had to lop his own toe off due to frostbite, and the time he'd been attacked by coons. Wilbur had been there with him through thick and thin, eighteen years or more, and though the temptation had often been there to simply give up and have a nice bacon sandwich, Larry had always managed to fight the urge to cook his little pal, since that would leave just him and his mother.

Edie Travers was a good mother, as far as Larry was concerned, but there were times when he wished she would just give up and leave him and Wilbur to live their lives in relative peace.

Take last week, for instance. Larry had been stung by a hornet while walking the pig through the woods. It had hurt like hell, but when Larry had revealed it to his mother, she'd panicked and gone to town on it. "Fetch me the vinegar!" she'd screeched. "And the baking soda...and the meat tenderiser. Oh, and a potato and some ammonia." Larry wasn't sure what she intended to do with all that, so off he went, expecting a nice soup. But when he returned, she slathered it all over him, leaving him looking like something that had just escaped from Cannibal Island.

There was something inherently wrong with a sixty-five year-old man being beaten to within an inch of his life with a meat tenderiser in the name of pain relief, by his eighty-nine year-old mother, no less.

Yes, life would be better once she'd kicked the proverbial bucket. Larry had a special plot picked in the woods for when the time came. She didn't know that, of course. That was the kind of thing that would freak the old bag out, and if she found out about it, she'd make his life a living nightmare for the years she had remaining.

"People can live to a hundred," Larry told Wilbur, patting her on the belly. She hated when he did that, but she'd seen the look he sometimes got in his eyes, the one often accompanied by a lick of the lips and a groaned "Mmmmmm." It wasn't worth grunting her disapproval, lest she become sausages. "Can you believe that shit? A *hundred.* That would mean Mother might live for another..." He took his socks off and counted his toes. Nine. Realising he didn't have enough digits, he slipped his socks back on and said, "More than nine years."

Wilbur sighed. It wasn't something many pigs could do, but this one had had plenty of practice over the years. She grunted once, just out of habit.

"No, I couldn't kill her," Larry said. "She's my *ma.*"

Wilbur grunted again. The English translation was: "I didn't suggest anything of the sort. You know what, silly nine-toed human? You really are a motherfucking waste of air."

"Put a pillow over her face while she *sleeps*?" Larry said, shocked and appalled in equal measure. "Wilbur, that's not very nice. She's been a mother to you, too. I know she sometimes kicks you, but she doesn't mean anything by it. She's just more of a squirrel person."

Wilbur sighed again. Plenty of practice...

"No, this is it for us, my little porker." Larry sighed. He'd had just as much practice as the pig. "No trouble. Nothing to worry about, apart from those strange worm-y things in my poo. Life could be worse." Could have been a damn sight better, too, but you play with the hand your dealt. If only Larry hadn't been dealt from a pack of *Happy Families*.

"I'm going in, now," Larry told Wilbur. The pig grunted: *thank fuck for that*. "Oh, don't be like that. I'll be back out to check on you before dark. Try not to shit until then. I'm not as young as I used to be."

He left the pig to wallow in its own filth and headed into the cabin, to where Edie Travers was cooking up a storm in the kitchen-cum-bathroom.

"You spend more time with that damn pig than you do with me," she said. It was water off a duck's back to Larry, who had to listen to the same diatribe on a daily basis.

"What does that tell you, Ma," Larry said, pulling his chair up to the table.

"You ain't too old for a whooping, Larry Travers," his mother said, spooning some unsightly concoction into an already dirty bowl. Some of it sloshed over the side and landed on the floorboards with the squelch. Larry watched as a cockroach scuttled toward it, had a little sniff, and then scurried away in the opposite direction, squeaking audibly. When the bowl was full, she turned from the stove and plonked it down in front of her son. "Ain't got no bread. You're gonna hafta drink it."

I'm going to have to kill it first, Larry thought, staring down into his bowl. "Thanks, Ma," he said, sticking his spoon into it and took his hand away. It stood up straight; never a good sign.

Edie Travers made herself a bowl and sat down opposite Larry. "Don't make any plans for tomorrow," she said as she pulled something that looked like a tail from the broth.

"Why?" Larry hated to ask, but it was best to find out now and come to terms with it, whatever it was.

"I found something in the toilet, and it wasn't one of mine. You got the worms, boy. We're gonna get those nasty sonsofbitches out of you before they eat your kidneys. Can't have my boy walking around with half-eaten kidneys. Nosiree. I've got myself a length of fishing-wire and a rabbit's foot. Old remedy, sort ya right out."

That was it. Larry had had enough. "I'm sick of being treated like a ten year-old boy," he said, so suddenly that Edie's false tooth fell out and landed in her soup with a *plonk!*. "I'm sixty-five. It should be up to me if I want to keep my worms or not."

Edie fished around in her bowl – using her fingers, of course, despite the spoon in her desiccated hand – and retrieved the tooth. Pushing it back onto the peg in her jaw, she said, "Nobody likes to *keep* worms, Larry, you poor, dumb asshole." That was her affectionate term for him. "No, we'll get them out of you before you can say *Ouch, that's a hair!*"

Larry shook his head. "*No*, Ma. I'm sick and tired of this. Wilbur and I have been talking and, well, things can't go on like this. If I don't kill something soon, I'm going to go crazy."

"What are you talkin' about, boy?" Edie said, sucking soup from her bony, spiderlike fingers. "Whatever that pig's putting into that thick skull of yours, it ain't true. It ain't never liked me."

Larry pushed his bowl away like a petulant child. When his mother pushed it back, he batted it off the table and across the room, to where it smashed into hundreds of pieces and its contents dripped down the bathroom wall.

Edie was furious, but she knew better than to engage with Larry when he was in a bad mood. She silently stood, walked across the room, and began to collect jagged porcelain shards, clinking and clanking more than a robot orgy.

"I'm sorry, Ma," Larry said. "I just...I've been giving this a lot of thought, and it's about time I did some real damage again."

"No, no, no, I don't wanna hear it—"

"It's time for Pigface to make a comeback." There. He'd said it. And it felt *good* to have said it.

His mother dropped the broken bowl pieces and turned her attention to Larry. "Son, ya got your ass set on fire. Wasn't that enough of a hint to retire? It's been almost forty years since ya last went up there, and you were lucky to get away with it then. What ya gonna do now? Hit 'em over the head with your walking stick until they stop breathing? Bore them to death with ya wartime tales?"

"I've still got the axe," Larry said, immediately regretting it as soon as he saw his mother's face drop.

"Ya been keepin' a murder weapon under this roof all this time?" She climbed up from her knees, apparently unaware that several pieces of bowl jutted bloodily out. "Boy, that hasta be one of the dumbest things you've ever done."

Larry had found the axe embedded in a tree down by Craven Road. That was in 1980, two full years after the tricky bitch had set him on fire up at Camp Diamond Creek. Even then he knew it was a sign, an indication he wasn't quite done with the massacring, not just yet. The years had gone by, and the itch had become almost impossible not to scratch.

"It was MY axe!" Larry said, remembering what the final girl had told him just before turning him into a charred caricature of himself. "I wasn't leaving it down there for any Tom, Dick, or Harry to find."

"Looks like a Dick found it anyway!" Edie said, returning to her chair. "No, killing's not for you, son, not anymore. Have ya thought about needlecraft? Hm? Perhaps a nice puzzle? You're spending too much time with that pig of yours. No wonder you're always edgy."

Edgy? That wasn't the word for it. Downright murderous, now that described it perfectly. He hadn't killed anyone in thirty-six years. The bubonic plague had better stats than him.

"I've got to get this out of my system," Larry said. "If I don't, there's no telling *what* I might do." He glowered at her. His own mother, and he was giving her a death-stare, hoping she would get the gist of what he was saying.

Of course, he wouldn't *really* hurt her, but he didn't need *her* to know that.

"Don't be giving me those evils, you little prick," Edie said, nonchalantly fingering her soup. "I pushed ya from my womb, and I'm not afraid to put ya back there." It made no sense, but Larry felt sick all the same. "Ya go on up to that camp after all this time, those kids are gonna make fun of you. Mark my words, no good will come of it." She poked a finger across the table at him; a wing of some description slipped from her knuckle and landed in the fruit bowl (which hadn't seen fruit in almost twenty years).

Larry took a deep breath. "Okay, Ma," he said, sucking the juice from her knobbly old finger. "You're right. I was a great killer, once upon a time. Now I can't even sneeze without pissing down my leg." He pushed his face into something resembling a smile. At least, it felt like a smile to him, but looked like something altogether creepier to Edie Travers.

"That's my boy," his mother said. A stringy hunk of meat had wrapped itself around her solitary tooth. It dangled from her mouth like a tampon string. "You don't wanna be gettin' into all that killin' again. Things have changed. Kids have got the smarts, now, and you've got the worms. Ya best off gettin' a hobby. Build me something nice in the garden. I've always wanted a sauna."

The thought of his mother's leathery body wrapped in steam, bits swinging this way and that, was too much. He excused himself from the table and went out to check on Wilbur. When the pig saw him, he mistook its grunt for joy. What it had actually said was:

Not this fucking guy again.

5

Camp Diamond Creek – 2014

"Oh, heyell no," Lakresha said as she stepped into the cabin that she and Junior would be calling home for the next week. If Jason had been in real estate, he would have said something along the lines of: *This is a very spacious room, if you're a Borrower or one of those little people with big heads. On your right you will see a lovely mirror covered in stunning cobwebs, and on your left you will see a wonderful king-size bed that looks as if it's been beautifully shat in by the entirety of the Harlem Globetrotters.* Since he wasn't in real estate, though, he said:

"I admit, things have gone a little bit downhill in recent years. We don't get many kids up here, not since the...well, not since I've been here."

"How many counsellors are up here?" Melissa said, pushing her way into the cabin.

"Including me?" Jason said, picking a dead rat up from the corner of the room and tossing it outside.

"Including you," Bailey said, stepping into the cabin. He didn't like rats, dead or alive.

"One," Jason said.

Freddy almost choked on his own tongue. "You're on your *own* up here? They left *you* in charge?"

"Nobody likes to work up here," Jason said, picking up a dead armadillo and hefting it out the window, which was more of a hole in the side of the cabin due to the lack of glass. "They're all over at the new resort a mile away. Don't know what all the fuss is about. It's like they've never seen a fifty-foot swimming pool before. I mean, what's the fucking point in twenty-five snooker tables, anyway? And don't even get me started on the health spa. As if campers want to spend their time being pampered and primped. That's not even camping. That's glamping!"

"That's where *we're* going," Lakresha said, pushing past Jason. It took Junior, Bailey, and Melissa to stop her from running for the van. "Didn't you fools hear what the man said? Heaven's just a mile away, and we're in some sort of filthy limbo."

"I've done some calculations," Cedric said, removing his glasses and wiping the lenses on the front of his tee-shirt, which said NEVER TRUST AN ATOM – THEY MAKE UP EVERYTHING. "This place is on ten acres, and there are seven of us, not including our host over there, which means we have one point four two acres each. Jason, how large is the new resort?"

Jason, still wearing the bottom half of a gorilla, shrugged. "It's about the same as this place, but two of those acres are the golf course."

"And how many people are over there right now?"

"A rough guess? Three hundred, plus fifty counsellors. It's very popular, for some reason."

Cedric smiled knowingly. "So that's ten acres, minus two for the golf course, so eight acres with three-hundred-and-fifty bodies. That's nought point nought two acres per person, if they're all spread out equally, which they won't be."

"What's your point, Hawking?" Bailey said, snorting.

"My *point* is that we have this whole place to ourselves, and that includes the creek from here down to the main road. Over at the new resort, you'd need to take a pregnancy test every night, such is the close proximity."

"He's right," Freddy said.

"He's *always* right," Amanda added. "That's why we keep him around."

"So, what? We're just going to stay here in this shit-hole?" Bailey said, peeling paint from the wall. Luckily, it snapped off when it did, otherwise the whole place would have come tumbling down.

"It's really not that bad," Jason said, but he was carrying what looked like half a chipmunk across the room; they couldn't really trust his opinion. "And think about it. You've got the run of the place. That's everything from here to the dead horse just along the creek."

"There's a dead horse just along the creek?" Junior asked, trying to remain calm.

Jason frowned. "I *think* it's a horse. It's been there a long time. Could be *anything*, I suppose."

"That's it," Lakresha said, dragging Junior toward the door. "Y'all can stay here in Camp Dumb'n'Crap, but we're out of here."

Junior took a few steps with his girlfriend before digging his heels in. The look she shot him would have killed most humans. "Baby, I think we should stay here," he said, timidly, shielding his face as if Lakresha might suddenly explode. Maybe she *would*. She was fierier than Satan's nutsack even when she was in a good mood.

"You want to stay here?" she said, hands on hips. "You want to stay here with all these dead things, in a cabin a Syrian refugee would politely decline?"

Jason scooped a handful of indeterminate droppings from one of the empty shelves. "You don't have to stay *here*," he said, examining one of the miniature shit-balls up close. He had no idea what he was looking for, but it made sense to at least appear to know what he was doing. "I just thought you'd each like your own space. If you don't mind kicking in together, the main cabin was recently rebuilt and in much better shape than these little cabins."

"How recently?" Freddy said.

"1979," Jason said. "Which isn't that long ago, if you class the nineties as what they were. A complete waste of time."

Freddy turned to Amanda with raised eyebrows; Amanda turned to Cedric, who shrugged; Cedric turned to Melissa, who didn't want to look at him for too long at the risk of being sick; Melissa turned to Lakresha, who turned to Junior, who completely ignored Bailey since the jock was too busy flexing his biceps to notice they were all sharing a moment.

"Let's go take a look at the main cabin," Freddy said.

Jason smiled. He could sell rice to the Chinese, ice to the Eskimos, and white American children to Angelina Jolie if he had to.

"Right this way," he said, hurling the droppings through the hole in the wall. "Watch your step. There are some dead critters out here."

*

If luxury was a country, and the little cabins were Afghanistan, the main cabin was Dubai. There was plenty of room for them to all sleep, and a gathering of sofas and chairs in the centre which were perfect for lounging around and playing cards/monopoly/fart-lighting. There were no beds, since the main cabin was designed more as a hub, a place for friends to meet up before embarking on whatever adventure they had planned. But Jason, being the kind half-gorilla he was, offered to deliver sleeping bags later that evening. There was no TV, but there was a CD player, and that was all they needed of an evening. Plus, Freddy had brought his acoustic guitar along, which meant they could all have a sing-song. All-in-all, they'd done very well for themselves. Even

Lakresha looked pleased. At least, she looked less *displeased*.

"Now *this* is what I'm talking about," Junior said, dropping his bag at the door and making a dart for the sofa. He misjudged his trajectory, and a moment later picked himself up from the rug in the middle of the cabin. "We'll take it."

"That's wonderful news," Jason said. "Any chance I can use the bathroom for a minute just to get this gorilla ass off? My balls are swimming."

They all nodded. Amanda tried not to vomit.

"Great. Then I'll get out of your way. Let you get settled in. I'll leave your sleeping bags just outside the door. In the meantime, you reprobates start enjoying yourselves. This is a summer camp, not a funeral parlour." Though there were enough dead things scattered around for it to qualify as the latter.

Jason disappeared through a door at the side of the room, squeezing his bulky bottom-half through with very little room for error. Once he was out of earshot, Bailey said:

"Asshole."

"C'mon man," Junior said. "He didn't have to give us this place. Seems like a dude to me."

"Well, if you go missing in the middle of the night," Bailey said, "we all know where to find you. In Jason's bed, sucking his balls." He laughed like a hee-hawing donkey, but he was the only one.

"Can't believe we're the only ones up here," Freddy said, changing the subject before things got nasty. "How awesome is that?"

"Have you stopped to think *why* we're the only ones up here?" Cedric said, ever the pessimist, always the buzz-kill. "And why the counsellors hate working here."

"The place is a *mess*," Lakresha said. "That's not reason enough?"

"Yeah, but it's the middle of summer," Cedric pressed. "This place should be teeming with people. It was cheap enough, and I don't care how luxurious and magnificent the new resort is, this place has a lot of character."

"Yeah," Lakresha said. "And that character is *Leatherface*." She started to unpack her first bag; the rest were down by the van, where no-one would steal them since there was no-one else about. It was doubtful they were going to get down there only to find a gang of rogue beavers making off with her Estee Lauder.

"A lot of businesses are failing in this industry," Cedric said. "Maybe Diamond Creek's going the same way."

"Well, at least we got in before it all went south," Amanda said. She didn't care how dilapidated it was, or that they were all going to be huddled together in the main cabin for the duration. She planned to sleep beneath the stars, anyway. Alone with her thoughts, with her mind, with nature. She couldn't hug trees with everyone else around; she needed her own space, and something to get the splinters out with afterwards.

"This is going to be epic!" Bailey said, passing a football from one hand to the other. "Go long, geek!"

Cedric didn't have time to 'go long' before the ball smashed him in the face, skewing his glasses and popping several pimples. *Yeah, epic*, Cedric thought as he straightened his specs. If nothing else, it was going to be an experience none of them would ever forget.

6

A Ramshackle Cabin – 2014

The heat in Larry's basement was unbearable, which meant there was a bad smell, too, though from *what*, he couldn't fathom. Something had clearly died down there, and was now violating his sanctuary. It was worse than Wilbur's pen. Much worse. Like centuries-old cheese wrapped in a gigolo's foreskin.

Larry was used to bad smells. You had to be if you wanted to be taken seriously as a serial slasher. It was no good killing someone and then spritzing the body and immediate area with lemon freshener afterwards. No, you had to become acclimatised to the stench of death, to inhale it regularly, the same way butchers inhaled the meat in a slaughterhouse.

With Larry, it was the other way round. He was actually *missing* the smell of death, the unmistakeable aroma of sliced teenager drifting along on the breeze. It was like a drug to him – a very addictive drug that, after thirty-six years, called out to him once again.

There was only one way he was going to stop the urge building up inside, and that was to go on a kill-crazy rampage. He could control it no longer.

And why should he? It was him, it was what he did, it was how he'd become famous, if only for a period back in the 1970s. But still...

"They won't be expecting it," he muttered to himself as he pulled the axe down from the wall and began to sharpen it. It felt good in his hand; like the first time a kid realises his penis isn't just for pissing through. He could still smell the blood on it from 1978, despite cleaning it religiously – every Sunday for the last thirty-six years.

Once the blade was nice and sharp, he placed it down on the wooden crate he liked to work from and smiled. Yes, this was going to work out very well, indeed.

He made his way to the back of the room and removed the shortest plank.

There it was. Slightly melted, but still very much recognisable; it was the mask that made him. He took it out and turned it over, so that the eyeholes gazed up at him; empty for now, but not for long.

"Squeeee!" he said, trying to contain his excitement. His erection pushed against his fly-hole, and it hurt like a sonofabitch, but it didn't last long. As a sixty-five year-old man, prolonged hard-ons were few and far between.

He lifted the mask so that it was level with his own face. "We're going to have some fun," he told it. "Just like old times."

But you've got a busted hip, the mask squealed, or *didn't*, Larry could never be sure what was real and what wasn't. All he knew was that it was rude to ignore the thing.

"I can still do this. WE can still do this." He fingered the nostril-holes as if he'd stumbled across a pair of Taiwanese twins in the woods.

Didn't you just have a heart-attack?

"That was years ago," Larry said. "And it was barely even a six on the Richter scale. My heart's stronger than it's ever been before."

I've been behind that wall for a helluva long time, the mask whined. *You sure you've still got the balls?*

Larry nodded. "Oh yeah. Granted, they're not as furry as they used to be, and one of them has slipped down a few inches, but they're both still there." He slipped the mask over his head; a spider, wondering what the fuck was going on, exited through one of the eyeholes and scrambled across the crate. The inside of the mask smelt like a rubber asshole, but Larry didn't even notice. He picked up the axe, and for the first time in decades he felt complete.

He didn't have a mirror – he was a serial murderer, not a Versace model – and so he gazed at his blurred image in the blade of his axe. "Looking good," he said, winking at himself. The eye beyond the eyehole thinned to a slit before opening again.

Your head's shrunk, the mask said.

"Lost some hair," Larry replied. "Happens to the best of us." The mask was starting to annoy him; had it always been so fucking talkative? Had it ever talked before? He cast his mind back to 1978. Nope, he couldn't recall it speaking to him then. This was a new thing. Another one of those things that only comes with age, like a weak bladder, dodgy hips, and a year's subscription to *People's Friend.*

So when are we going out? the mask asked, enthusiastically. *I want to see some blood, some bare breasts, some bloody bare breasts...*

"All in good time," Larry told the overzealous mask. "Ma doesn't know about this, and telling her would *kill* her. We're going to have to be *extremely* careful." By careful, he meant waiting for his mother to go to bed before heading up to the camp.

Holy shit, is she still alive? The mask asked, incredulous. *Yo momma's so old, her birth certificate expired!*

"Yes, yes, she's—"

Yo momma's so old, her social security number is 1...

"Yeah, look, can we not do—"

Yo momma's so old, she knew the Burger King when he was just a prince...

"That's enough, you masky cunt!" Larry's patience was thinner than a gnat's scrotum stretched over a fifty-gallon drum. He tore the mask from his head, forgetting for a moment that he had a beard.

You've left some hair in me, the mask said.

"I can *see* that," Larry replied, pulling out silver hairs by the handful. "Look, from now on I'd appreciate it if you only speak when spoken to."

Fine, the mask said. *I'll do that if you promise to have a breath mint before you wear me again.*

"Deal," Larry said. He had no idea what a breath mint was, nor where he would get one from at such short notice, but the mask was in no position to make deals. "I'm going to put you away for a while. I don't know how long it will be, but just be prepared."

Be prepared, the mask repeated. *Got you. I'll be in my hole if you need...*

The voice trailed off as Larry stuffed the pig mask back into the space he'd retrieved it from and covered it over with the loose plank. *Well that's just charming, that is...how many years since I last saw him, and he gives me two minutes of bad breath and a promise he probably won't keep...*

"Pipe down in there," Larry said, never once considering the fact that he was talking to himself. "If *she* finds you, there's no telling what she might do." He had a feeling it would involve a box of matches and a litre of kerosene.

After hanging the axe back in its proper place on the wall, he climbed the steps leading up to the shed and locked the whole thing up with seven deadbolts and three padlocks. If his mother did come snooping, she'd have to work for it, though she didn't, Larry thought, have the hands for lock-picking. It would be like trying to thread a needle with gloves made of ginger root.

It was starting to get dark. In the distance, an owl hooted, and Larry's erection returned with a vengeance...for about eight seconds.

7
Camp Diamond Creek – 2014

"Kum-bah-yah my Lord, Kum-bah-yah. Kum-bah-yah my Lord, Kum-bah-yah. Kum-bah-yah my Lord, Kum-bah-yah... you know, this is awfully repetitive," Cedric said. "I don't suppose you know anything else?"

They were all sitting in the living area, surrounding by bottles of wine and cans of beer. Freddy was strumming his guitar as if he knew what he was doing. The truth was, he only knew three chords, but that had never stopped Status Quo or Oasis.

"That's a *classic* camping song," Freddy said, tucking his plectrum behind the strings. His fingers were already sore; he needed a break before he broke the skin.

"I can't be doing with that shit," Bailey said, crushing a can against his forehead. Trouble was, the can was only half-empty. Beer went everywhere. Bailey didn't seem to notice; he was too busy cracking open the next one. After sucking the foam from it, he said, "What else do you know?"

Freddy swallowed hard. He hadn't anticipated such a tough crowd. *I'll bet the Arctic Monkeys don't get this shit.* "We've got the whole world in our hands?"

"Shit," Bailey said. "Next."

"Erm...I love the mountains?"

"Shit. Dude, you know what? Give me the damn guitar." He held out a hand; Freddy was reluctant to put anything in it, and his expression said as much. "Come on, bitch, I won't break it."

Freddy sighed. The guitar had been a gift from his mother. Did he *really* want to hand it to the guy who had almost blown them all to kingdom come? Did he really have a *choice*? Bailey was twice the size of him, and a lot fitter. If he wanted the guitar, he could just take it. Best to do it the easy way.

Sorry Mom...

"Thanks, Clapton," Bailey said as Freddy passed the instrument over. "Now, this is how it's done."

What happened next was something for the record books. Freddy had never seen all six strings break on a downward stroke before, but somehow Bailey had managed it. He stared out at the others, his fingers still trembling, the guitar still making an awful noise, even though it was *sans* strings.

"Nice one, asshole," Amanda said, shaking her head. "Decided to skip the song and go straight for the destruction. Nice." She shot him the devil horns.

"Cheap guitar," Bailey said, handing the wrecked instrument back to Freddy, who looked at it as if he'd never seen one before. In a way, he hadn't. Not one like this.

"Now what?" Lakresha said, pouring herself a large glass of brandy. "And the first one of y'all fuckers to mention strip poker is going to wish they hadn't."

Cedric backed away from the group, slipping the deck of cards back into his trouser pocket.

"Anyone know any scary stories?" Junior said, lighting what could only be described as a joint big enough to put Seth Rogen on his back.

"Come on," Melissa said, shaking her head. "That stuffs for kids and retards. We've heard them all a thousand times before."

"*I've* got one," Jason said. Somehow, he had become part of their little group. It seemed only fair to let the guy stick around for a few hours. He had, after all, brought them something to sleep in.

"Don't tell me," Lakresha said. "It's the one about the woman in black who haunts the railway. Or the one about the head bouncing on the roof of that dumbass couple's car? Or the one about Michael Jackson and how he managed to get away with murder for all those years."

Jason shook his head. "This one's much scarier than all of those combined." He reached across and poured a large glass of whiskey before settling into his armchair.

"It happened in 1956..."

8
Camp Diamond Creek – 1956

It was a warm, summer's day; so hot that kids were doing whatever they could to avoid direct sunshine, lest they return to their parents at the end of the week, only for their parents to turn around and say, "That one's not mine. Mine's white." To keep out of the sun, the majority of the campers had headed into the woods, where the branches and leaves offered generous protection. Games were played, some of them bordering on illegal – someone had even started a fire – and everyone was having fun.

Everyone except for little Larry Travers.

Larry Travers was a good kid, but he felt lost without his mother. This was the first time they'd been apart since she pushed him kicking and screaming into the world seven years ago, and while he liked to play silly games as much as the next kid, he preferred to play them with his mother, and not a bunch of asshole stranger-kids.

Sitting at the edge of the creek, dipping his toes in the water, Larry prayed that the week would be over soon, so that he could return home, to where his mother would wash him, and kiss him, and tell him how brave he'd been for going off to camp all by his lonesome.

Home was a small house not too far from the Diamond Creek. It was the kind of place you wouldn't look at twice if you drove past it, and that was exactly how Larry and his mother liked it. There was no

Mr Travers – Larry's father had run from the hospital on the morning of Larry's birth, leaving Edie Travers pushing, sweating, and farting and wondering what the hell she was going to do for money now that her coward husband had decided to leave her.

When Larry came out, she'd grabbed onto the umbilical cord with the intention of tying it around both their throats until death stole them away. As it turns out, umbilical cords aren't as long as one might expect.

She had told Larry that story over and over, usually at bedtime, because there was nothing more heart-warming or sleep-inducing than a tale of attempted infanticide. Larry would listen, never daring to ask the reasons why she didn't do it. Then his mother would kiss him three times; once on the forehead, once on the nose, and then once on the lips. It was the lips one that smelt the worst, but if Larry held his breath just as she kissed his forehead...

"Look at what we've got over here," a voice said. Larry almost fell into the creek. "It's that weird kid. Hey, weird kid, why don't you come hang out with us?"

Larry glanced across his shoulder and saw the three boys, almost twice his size and certainly a few years older than him. One of them was wearing a blue and red argyle-pattern sweater, and Larry couldn't help thinking the boy was an idiot, since it was hotter than the surface of the sun, or close enough.

"I'm okay here," Larry said, gesturing to the creek. He didn't want to 'hang out' with these boys. He didn't want to hang out with *anyone*. He wanted to be left alone so that he could think about his mother in peace.

"Aw, don't be like that," another of the boys said. This one was...what was the word for it? *Portly.* Yes, this one was a fat fucker, with beads of sweat dripping down his forehead, and quite a large forehead it was, too. "We're just trying to be polite, ain't we boys?"

They both concurred. "That's right," Argyle said. "You look like you could do with some friends, and that's why we're here." He smiled to reveal a mouthful of popcorn teeth. "Come on, we're only exploring. How far down the creek did you go? I'll bet it goes all the way to the moon."

"Yeah, the moon," Fat Fuck said.

The third boy finally decided to join in. "But the m-m-m-moon's not *safe*," he said. "My d-d-d-daddy says there won't ever be a-a-a-a-a man on the m-m-m-moon."

"Your daddy don't know *shit*, Stutters" Argyle said. Turning back to Larry, he said, "So what do you say, kid? Want to come exploring with us?"

For some odd reason, Larry knew they wouldn't take no for an answer. The only way to get rid of them was to give them what they wanted, at least for a few minutes. He could make his excuses and leave once he'd had enough.

Larry picked himself up from the bank and put his socks and shoes back on. "We're not going far, are we?" he said, trying to tie his shoelaces. He couldn't, and so tucked them into his socks, just like his mother taught him.

"No, not far at all," Fat Fuck said. "There's this really swell place we want to show you. We found it yesterday. I think you're gonna love it."

Larry liked the sound of that. He liked swell places, but he liked them even more when he wasn't with other kids. "What is it?" he said, sidling up alongside the older boys. "Some sort of abandoned building."

Stutters grinned. Unlike Argyle, his teeth were all one colour. Pity the colour was green. "Oh, it-it-it-it's not aba-aba-abandoned," he said.

Scratching his head, Larry followed the boys along the creek. He hoped they didn't go as far as the moon. From what he'd heard, the atmosphere was terrible there. Plus, he didn't even *like* cheese.

"This way, weird kid," Argyle said, climbing up an incline. Dirt and rocks toppled behind him, a mini-avalanche of woodland floor.

"It's *Larry*," Larry said, though he had no idea why. Weird kid was perhaps more appropriate.

"Larry," Fat Fuck said.

"L-L-L-L-Larry," Stutters added. "S-s-s-swell name."

"Thanks," Larry said. He hated his name, since people always expected him to be happy. His mother called him *Son* a lot, which he preferred, but he couldn't ask these three boys to call him that. Might sound a bit weird. "How much farther is it?"

Argyle, panting like a thirsty dog, said, "Just at the top of this hill." He put his hand down his shorts and had a good ol' rake around. "Trust me, it's worth it."

"W-w-w-worth it," Stutters said, but there was something about the way he said it that worried Larry. All of a sudden, he wished he'd told them no, that he was fine where he was – *I did! I did say that!* – but it was too late now.

Didn't go with the nice boys up the hill to see the swell place? his mother's voice said, mockingly. *I don't know why I didn't just call you Laura and be done with it...*

At the top of the hill was a small clearing. Beyond that was a small ramshackle cabin that looked like nothing Larry had ever seen before. This wasn't like the nice cabins down at the camp; this cabin had been built by hand – a very unsteady hand, by the looks of it. Bits leaned this way, planks leaned that, and the whole structure looked as if it would all come crashing down if anyone sneezed too close to it.

"What is it?" Larry asked. "Other than swell?"

Argyle, Fat Fuck, and Stutters were all in a line, now, staring back at him. Something had changed about them. Gone were the friendly multi-coloured smiles; they'd been replaced by intent gazes, and Larry didn't like it one bit.

"Okay boys," Argyle said, removing his sweater. Fat Fuck took off his tee-shirt to reveal tits bigger than Larry's mother's. Stutters eventually got his shirt off, too; it seemed his impediment went further than just speech. Larry stood watching, not knowing what they were doing, or what they were going to do next. If he'd known, he might have had time to run, to call out for one of the counsellors, but by the time the thought crossed his mind, it was too late.

"Grab him!" Fat Fuck said, lurching toward him like something from Forbidden Planet. Larry turned to run, but Argyle was on him in a second, dragging him to the ground, sweaty belly rubbing against the back of Larry's head.

"Grab his legs," Argyle said, and then a second later, Larry's legs were very much grabbed. Then something was rammed into his mouth, something sweaty and rancid; it didn't take long for Larry to figure out that it was a sock. Stutters' one bare foot was a dead giveaway.

Mumbling at them, warning them that his mother wouldn't be too happy when she heard about this, Larry could only watch as the treetops passed by overhead; the occasional snippet of sunlight breaking through and hitting him directly in the eyes.

Then Argyle made a noise above him. "Squeeeeee!" he said, whatever the hell that meant.

"Sq-sq-sq-sq-squeeee!" Stutters said as he walked alongside his pals.

Larry closed his eyes and accepted his fate, whatever that may be. These were big boys – older boys – and they would do with him what they pleased. He just hoped it didn't involve a cucumber and a pot of honey.

"This little piggy went to market," Argyle said.

"This little piggy stayed home," Fat Fuck sang.

"This little p-p-p-p-p-p-p-p-p-p-p-p-p-p—"

"For fuck's sake, Stutters," Argyle reproached. "If you can't manage it, stay out of the song."

Larry moaned as the tumbledown cabin appeared overhead.

"This little piggy had roast beef," said Argyle.

"And this little piggy had none," added Fat Fuck.

And then they were swinging him, leg-and-a-winging him high, and laughing like hyenas as they did so.

"And this little piggy cried wee-wee-wee-wee-wee..."

They let go on the upswing. Larry spun through the air. Since he weighed less than four stone wringing wet, he went high — almost level with the cabin's rotten roof — before gravity decided to make an appearance. He landed face down in what, at first glance, appeared to be mud. There was a squelch, and then Larry couldn't breathe.

"All the way home," one of the boys said. Then they all laughed in unison. It was one of the worst sounds Larry had ever heard.

He pulled his face out of the mud, and that was when the stench hit him. An ungodly scent that could only be described as *shitty*. Quickly, he scraped away the thick, brown stuff from his eyes and removed his shirt, which he then used to wipe his face with.

"Look!" Argyle said from somewhere to Larry's right. "We found you some friends." Then they all laughed again.

Larry could finally open his eyes, and as soon as he did, he wished he hadn't.

He was surrounded by pigs. There must have been twenty, maybe thirty in total, and they were all grunting and *squeeee*-ing, climbing over one another to get to him.

"He's pissed his pants!" Fat Fuck said, pointing at the blossoming damp patch on

Larry's shorts. Larry wished the ground would open up and swallow him, put him out of his misery, but it didn't.

What happened next was much, much worse.

The pigs reached him, and all Larry remembered was an immense weight above him, and the occasional excited *squeee* as the animals all piled on. He screamed, but no one would have heard him, not beneath all that swine.

"Come on," Larry heard Argyle say to the others above the frantic grunts surrounding him. "Let's leave weird kid to his new friends."

Larry closed his eyes and thought of his mother.

What kind of kid follows a group of strangers up a hill to an old cabin, anyway? her voice chided. *A dumb one, that's who. Now get out from under those pigs before I have to come down there and drag you out by your ears.*

Larry cried and cried as he tried to pull himself free. For two hours he was trapped, and for an hour of that he had a pig's tail in his mouth (at least, he *hoped* it was a tail).

Then, he was free, dragging himself toward the fence at the edge of the sty. He could feel the pigs nibbling at his ankles, grunting at him to *Come back, weird kid. Come back and take it like a man!*

He threw a tired hand up at the fence and, half an hour later, landed in the grass on the other side, sobbing and gasping. As far as afternoons went, he'd had better.

On the way back to Camp Diamond Creek he vomited several times, once on his own knee. And no matter how hard he tried, he couldn't get the terrible noise out of his head.

Squeeeee...

Squeeeee...

Squ-cough-cough-cough-ahem-eeee...

9

Everyone was speechless. Freddy took a long gulp of beer as he let the story sink in. On the opposite sofa, Lakresha and Junior were engaging in a game of tonsil-tennis, one that neither of them seemed to be winning.

"Well *there's* fifteen minutes I'm never getting back," Melissa said, lighting a cigarette.

"That was pretty weak, dude," Bailey said. "I'm normally a huge fan of bullying stories, but that pig kid, he was kind of a fag."

Amanda, though, was intrigued. Sure, it was no David Copperfield, but the elements were all there for a decent TV adaptation. Maybe something for True Entertainment to consider. "Poor kid," she said, shaking her head.

"Unfortunately," Jason said, adopting what he considered to be a creepy voice (it actually sounded as if he was trying to stifle a bout of wind). "That was only the beginning."

"What happened next?" Freddy said. He wasn't overly interested, but Amanda seemed to be, and that was enough for him.

"*That* year? Nothing. Larry didn't see Fat Fuck, Argyle, or Stutters the rest of the week. I guess he went home to his mother, but the events of that terrible afternoon in the pig-sty must have left a scar."

"Pigs can do that," Cedric said. "Their jaws are stronger than any dog's. A fully-grown hog can crunch through a deer leg as if it's made of butter."

"Not a *physical* scar," Jason said. "No, this was mental. What happened to him fucked him up in the head. I'm talking full-on Gary Busey whacko. In 1975, Larry returned to Camp Diamond Creek with only one thing in mind."

"If this is a kiddy-fiddler story," Lakresha said through a mouthful of Junior's tongue, "I don't want to hear it."

"It's not." Jason sipped at his whiskey and grinned. "In 1975, Larry Travers donned a pig-mask for the very first time. He came into the camp in the dead of night and killed twenty-four campers, seven counsellors, and three clowns that the camp had hired for a Saturday morning matinee." He paused for effect, as was his wont. "Two ballerinas, a handful of furry mascots, and the camp pet, Gordon the Gecko."

Silence.

More silence.

Even more silence, and then Bailey finally said, "Bullshit."

Jason chortled. "It sounds far-fetched, but it's absolutely true. When he was finished killing everything in his path, Larry disappeared. In 1976, he came back and killed thirty-two, including an entire special-school. In '77, another thirty, and in 1978, he murdered a group of kids, twelve of them so nondescript that it took dental records to identify them."

"How did he keep getting away with it?" Amanda asked, frowning. "I mean, all those poor kids. Surely the camp would have done something about it."

"They put a sign up," Jason said. "But it went missing, and the camp decided it wasn't economically viable to have another one made."

"But the police *caught* him, right?" Cedric said. Suddenly, he wished he wasn't the one closest to the door.

Jason shook his head. "In 1978, Larry died in this very cabin. Obviously not *this* cabin, but the one that stood here before this one was built. The final girl – you're all familiar with the 'final girl' concept?"

They nodded in unison.

Jason smiled. Of *course* they were familiar with it. It was the bread-and-butter of survival horror stories. "She managed to lock him in the shitter and then burned the place down. They say that if you listen carefully, on really quiet nights, you can still hear him *squeeee*-ing as the rubber pig mask melts onto his face."

Freddy arched his eyebrows. A shiver crept down his spine. This Jason kid sure knew how to tell a good story, bullshit or not.

"When they finally managed to get the fire under control," Jason continued, "the police came in to find all these dead bodies charred to a crisp, but they never found Larry's remains. There was no sign of the pig mask he'd worn to slaughter a hundred people over the years; no sign at all he'd ever existed. It was as if he'd just...*disappeared*..." He left that last word trailing, hissing it like Donald Pleasance.

"Have you ever thought about applying for Sesame Street?" Junior said. "They'd *love* you."

Jason held up placatory hands. "Don't shoot the messenger. I'm just telling you what happened up here. You wanted a creepy story, what's creepier than the thought that Larry, the Pigface killer, is still out there somewhere, waiting, hoping for another shot at glory?"

Cedric had had enough. Standing, he moved away from the door, only to find that he was now the closest one to the window. *Fuckit!*

"And on that bombshell," Bailey said, pulling the ring on another beer, "Does anyone want to play strip-poker? I know the geek has a deck of cards."

Cedric's mouth fell open. "They're not playing cards," he said, flabbergasted. "It's my ultra-rare *Magic: The Gathering* deck, and no, I will not whip out my Abyssal Persecutor, or my Blightsteel Colossus."

"Thank fuck for that," Lakresha said, holding her thumb and forefinger an inch apart.

Cedric gave her the finger. "Oh, haha. You wouldn't be saying that if you saw my Baneslayer Angel."

"Honey, you bring your Baneslayer Angel anywhere near me and I'm gonna bite it off."

"I'm going to take a little walk," Amanda said, pushing herself up from the floor. Everyone looked at her as if she'd said *I'm going to go to the local kennel and kick puppies until my feet hurt.*

"Didn't you hear what my man Jay said?" Bailey started to roll something that definitely wasn't tobacco, unless they'd started making tobacco in green. "There's a nutty fuck out there wearing a pig mask, just waiting for some nubile young babe like you to hack up."

Amanda sighed. "Just a story," she said. "And even if it *did* happen, that was forty years ago, before any of us were born. The guy would be dead by now, or at least too old to go on another killing spree."

Freddy pushed up from the sofa. "I'll go with you," he said. "I mean, if you want me to. I could use some fresh air, and I think it's about to get very hazy in here." He gestured to the joint Bailey was working on.

Though she didn't seem too happy about it, Amanda said, "Come on, then. I want to see the moonlight glistening on the creek before it gets too cloudy."

"Sounds beautiful," Freddy said. What he wanted to see was the moonlight glistening on Amanda's naked and creek-drenched body, but you take what you can get.

Besides, it was a nice night for a walk.

And Freddy didn't really believe that Larry 'Pigface' Travers was still out there, roaming the camp, meting vengeance on people who had nothing at all to do with that fateful summer in 1956.

What kind of an idiot murderer would hang around for forty years after butchering so many people?

10
A Ramshackle Cabin – 2014

"You go to sleep now," Edie said, leaning down and kissing Larry, once on the forehead, once on the nose, and once on the lips/beard. She didn't have to lean as much as she used to; the natural arch of her aged, crooked figure made it a lot easier than it was, say, sixty years ago.

His room was an alcove under the kitchen sink. It was the kind of place a normal family would create for their Labradoodles, but Larry couldn't sleep anywhere else. Plus, it was close to his litter tray, in case he had to go doody in the night.

"Night, Ma," Larry said, as the crooked figure creaked its way across the room, into the shadows, where he saw her faint outline collapse into the armchair.

He knew he wouldn't have to wait long. His mother could sleep at the drop of a hat. Larry knew her routine better than she did. In a minute, she would pick up her needlework, Then she would prick her finger and say *Ouch, you spikey cunt!* before putting the hardly-started blanket down and pouring herself a large glass of shine. It wasn't the best shine, but it was enough to knock her out on a nightly basis. She would finish the glass, smack her lips together, and say *Tastes like shit!* which always surprised Larry. Of *course* it tasted like shit; she brewed it in the shithouse. Then she would put the glass down and pick up her book. Larry didn't know what she was reading at the moment, but it was something to do with all these different shades of grey. Sounded boring as hell to him, but his mother seemed to be enjoying it. At that point he would close his eyes, because he didn't like to see what she did with that pillar candle from the cupboard, the one that smelt odd. Then, two minutes later, she would put the book down and close her eyes, and then the snoring would start.

God, you've never heard someone snore so much. Ever since her nostrils sprouted hair like Chewbacca's ballsack, she'd made this horrible sound, like ships honking at one another. Tonight, though, that sound would be his signal.

"Ouch, you spikey cunt!" his mother said from the gloom.

Larry grinned.

Tonight was the nigh

11
The Creek – 2014

It was a nice night for a walk, but it would have been much nicer if they could see where they were fucking going. Neither of them had had the gumption to bring a torch, and so they'd spent the last half-an-hour wandering in circles, trying to figure out where the sound of the gently-drifting water was coming from. Freddy had considered offering his hand, lest they get separated, but had ultimately decided against it. He didn't want to come across as opportunistic. Plus his hands were clammy, and about as comforting as a bucket of wet fish.

"There it is," Amanda said. "Diamond Creek, the only known creek in the vicinity which bifurcates."

"Really?" Freddy said. "Dirty bastard."

As they walked toward it, everything became brighter. "No, that means it splits into two," Amanda sniggered. Even though Freddy couldn't see her face, he knew those beautiful dimples were there. Would she think it weird if he reached up and put his fingers into them, like a bowling ball? Probably.

"You really love this nature stuff, don't you?" Freddy said, tripping up over a low-lying branch. He picked himself up and caught up with Amanda, who apparently hadn't noticed his absence.

"...beautiful things in the world," she was saying. "You just have to know where to find them." Although he'd missed the first part of the speech, Freddy got the gist of it.

They stopped walking at the edge of the water. It would have been awfully silly to keep going.

"I've always been a big fan of trees," Freddy lied. "The way they...grow, and I like that they...are green...like...limes." *Okay, stop talking, Freddy. You're making a tit of yourself.*

"Trees are awesome," Amanda said. Freddy sighed with relief. "Did you know that in one day, one large tree can lift up to a hundred gallons of water out of the ground and discharge it into the air?"

Freddy did *not* know that, but he liked that *she* did. Amanda never pretended to be anything other than her true self; a nature-loving, tree-hugging, animal-nurturing, piss-drinking, barefoot-walking beauty. She was everything he wanted in a girl, and his mother wouldn't be unhappy if he should bring her home, providing Amanda didn't pull an empty glass from her hundred-percent vegan handbag and crouch over it right there in the living room.

"I just had to get out of there," Amanda said, barely more than a whisper, as if she was concerned a nosey beaver might hear and head back to the main cabin to throw her under the bus.

"I know," Freddy said. He, too, whispered, but had no idea why. "Like heroin, they're okay in small doses." Not the best analogy, but it was too late to take it back.

"I can't stand Bailey," she said, dropping onto her haunches and rifling through the dirt like some low-rent Indiana Jones. "And that girlfriend of his is just annoying."

"Yeah, they're not the quickest tractors on the farm," Freddy said, watching as Amanda picked something up, blew the dirt from it, and shoved it into her mouth. He tried not to gag, but suddenly his tonsils felt twice as big as they were a moment ago. "Ergh. Ergh. Ergh..."

"You okay?" She looked up at him, chewing frantically, like a grazing camel.

"I'm...fine," he lied. *Please don't spew on her head...please don't spew on her head...please don't...* "We had to invite them. He's Junior's best friend, and Lakresha gets on really well with Melissa."

"Because they're both materialistic whores," Amanda said, smiling. "Makes sense."

"Cedric's cool, though. In his own, geeky way."

"Yeah, I like him." She sifted through the dirt once more. Freddy looked away, taking deep breaths. If they ever *did* get together, he would have to have a word about her diet. Maybe if he carried a bag of nuts around with him whenever they went on a date...

They fell silent, simply enjoying the creek, just two people, not talking, not looking at each other, not knowing what would happen next, if anything.

Freddy liked it, though. It was nice. Not much fun, but nice all the same.

He just hoped he didn't end up in the friendzone, the only place in the world more tedious than the Alabama Button Museum.

12
A Ramshackle Cabin – 2014

He pulled the crisp, white apron over his head. It shouldn't have been crisp *or* white, but his mother had recently washed it. She'd even ironed it, removing some of his favourite creases. She was nothing if not thorough. He was almost certainly the best-dressed slasher/maniac out there. She'd even polished his boots, which were a lot tighter than the last time he'd worn them. It's amazing how fat one's feet can get in thirty-six years. He didn't know whether it was water retention, or if his toenails had grown funny. After five minutes of hopping around the basement, kicking the floor and scuffing his mother's beautiful handiwork, the boots were stretched just enough to bear.

Why are you limping? The pig mask asked as he took it from its hiding place. *Your hip gone already?*

"My hips are fine," Larry said, turning the mask over so that the eyeholes faced away from him. "*Ish.*" He was about to pull the mask over his head when it said:

Breathmint?

Larry sighed. "What did I say about speaking when spoken to?" The fact that the mask shouldn't have been speaking at *all* was not lost on him.

He pulled the mask down, being careful not to snag his beard on the rubber. He could still smell the burn on the inside of it, and was momentarily transported back to that terrible night in '78. How could he have been so stupid? To let that bitch trick him so easily? Well, that wouldn't happen again, not on your nelly. He was Pigface 2.0, forty years older and forty years wiser, though there's a limit on how wise you can get when you're living in a tumbledown hut in the middle of the woods.

With the mask adjusted so that his wiry moustache didn't block the snout-holes (a lesson he only learnt once he'd turned purple) Larry sat himself down at the small, wooden crate and began to write.

He wasn't great with words or letters, but he had an inkling into which order they went. His handwriting was atrocious, but mother would be able to read it.

Ma, he wrote. It was best to start off nice and simple, work his way up from that. *I cud not elp micelf. I no I sed I wud be gud, but I ad too get it owt of my cistern.* "Cistern?" he mumbled. "Yeah, close enough." *I just wont yu too no I luv yu, and ope that yu dont fink ill of me for wot I ave dun.*

Ah, that's fucking lovely, that is, the mask mocked. *You've forgotten to put kisses.*

"I haven't finished yet," Larry said, angrily. "And you mind your own business. Just because your mother was a tyre."

I fink this will bee the last tym I ave too do this, he wrote. *Im not getting eny yunger, and my best dayz of chaysing kids wiv an ax are beehynd me. I promis wunce this is ova, I will get an obby. Ive all ways fanseed dewing thows sewdowkews in the payper. Im not grayt wiv numbas, but Ill giv it a gow if it mayks yew happee.*

He wanted to see her happy. Just not as happy as she gets when she reads that weird book of hers at bedtime.

Sow, if yew fynd this letta befor I get bak from killin, I dont wont yew too wurry. Ive still got wot it tayks. I will mayk yew prowd, Ma. I promis. xxxxx

He read it back as best he could, rather pleased with himself. There were hardly *any* spelling mistakes. Maybe a crossword hobby wasn't beyond the realms of possibility, or a job writing subtitles for Fox News.

P.S. Thanx for iyoning my apron.

He left the note on the crate and took the axe down.

This is gonna be fun, the mask said. *Providing you don't have a coronary before we get to the top of the hill.*

13

Camp Diamond Creek – 2014

Midnight. The Witching Hour, when creatures of the night are purported to be at their most powerful, if you believed in that sort of nonsense. The clock on the mantelpiece chimed, its rusty innards barely managing to hold a note longer than Britney Spears without autotune.

"And *that*," Cedric said, relaxing back in his chair following his lengthy diatribe, "is why Superman and Wonder Woman would never have children."

There was a moment of silence; the atmosphere was thick enough to cut with a plastic spatula.

"Have you ever *kissed* a girl?" Bailey said, before erupting with laughter. Everyone joined in, including Jason, who wasn't even a *bona fide* member of the group.

Cedric wished he hadn't bothered. These weren't his target audience. His target audience were back at home, at this hour playing *Warcraft* and eating chips. They would have loved to hear about Superman's all-too-powerful gizz.

"You know what," Cedric said, standing and drunkenly teetering around for a while until he figured out where his feet were. "I don't have to take this sort of abuse." He moved for the door. At least he *thought* he did. Turns out that doors and refrigerators are interchangeable when intoxicated. It wasn't until the cold hit him that he realised his error.

He closed the fridge door and edged along the wall until he found what he was looking for. As he slipped out into the night, ignoring the raucous laughter behind him, his head began to spin. He removed his glasses and wiped them on the front of his tee-shirt, but that didn't help. He'd drunk too much, inhaled too much of Bailey's second-hand smoke, and now it was as if he was seeing everything through aquarium-tinted specs.

"Fucking assholes wouldn't know intellele...intellecle...*intellectual* conversation if it bit them on the ass." He walked slowly down the hill, sometimes on the gravel path, more often on the grass verge lining it.

Amanda. That's what he would do. He would find Amanda and Freddy. They were decent people. If they'd been in the cabin, they would have defended him. Where they hell had they gone off to? Why hadn't he gone with them when he'd had the chance, instead of sitting around the cabin talking to a bunch of bastards and getting inadvertently high?

He stopped staggering for a moment and unzipped his flies. Leaning one-handed against what he assumed was a tree, he began to piss. "Ahhhhhhhhhhhhhhhhhhhhhhhhhhhhhh," he said, smiling. It stung a little, but it was a nice pain, one that reminded him that this was all real, and not some dream brought on by his inebriation. Looking down at his shrivelled member as it pumped out litre after litre of urine, he thought about home, about the complete collection of *Star Wars* figures hanging on his bedroom wall, and about how happy they made him. He didn't need a girlfriend, not when he had a mint, carded, 1977 Princess Leia from Kenner. Oh, how he'd masturbated over that one.

Suddenly, something to his right moved. By the time he managed to snap his head across, there was nothing there. But he could hear...*something*. A wheezing from within the trees.

"Hello?" he said, zipping himself up even though he wasn't quite finished. "Amanda? Freddy? Is that you?"

The wheezing turned to coughing. Cedric was certain he heard a voice say, "Fucking steep hill," before the coughing returned.

"Guys, this isn't funny," he said, slowly walking toward the source of the noise. "I've got piss down my leg, now."

The trouble with drink is that it tends to fuck up your vision. Cedric could barely see as it was, since it was so dark, but what he *could* see was in triplicate, which only served to disorientate him further.

He stepped off the path and managed to traverse the first tree with only minor injuries. "Say something," he said. "I don't know where you are."

The wheezing was settling down, now. It was almost impossible to discern over the gentle wind rustling through the treetops above. Off in the distance, an owl hooted. If Cedric had brushed up on his owl-speak, he would have understood perfectly and got the hell out of there. Unfortunately, he hadn't, and so moved deeper into the trees, trying to fathom which ones were real and which were drunken mirages.

"If that's you, Amanda, I'm really disappointed. I thought you were different to the others." He didn't like the sound of his own voice. It was too nasally, far too whiny, and not at all the kind of voice that Amanda – or *any* woman, for that matter – would find attractive. "Come on out. This isn't funny." More pee trickled down his leg, and he cursed himself for not shaking before tucking himself away.

Just then, something rushed through the trees behind him, and he spun so fast and hard that he ended up sitting in an untidy pile.

That was when the figure emerged, the axe raised high, the pig-mask just visible through the gloom. "Squee-*cough*-squeee!" it wheezed, then lowered the axe. "Give me a minute. I'm absolutely fucked." The shape doubled over, panting for breath. "That hill...that hill has to be...the *worst* bit of landscaping...in the history of man."

Cedric climbed to his feet, frowning and squinting into the darkness. "Is that you, Freddy?" he said. It didn't sound like Freddy, but you could get those voice-changer thingamabobs. He had one at home that, when spoken into, altered his voice to sound like that of a dalek. At the flick of a switch, he could sound like a transformer, and another switch gave him the dulcet tones of Jennifer Tilly.

"Not...Freddy," Pigface said, holding up a hand to suggest he wasn't quite ready for a conversation. Eventually, he straightened up. "Phew. That's better. Now, where were we?"

"Junior, is that you?" Cedric slurred, stepping toward the masked figure. "Did Lakresha put you up to this?"

Larry had no idea who Lakresha was, or why any mother would call their child such a thing, but he needed the boy to come closer. He was too tired to chase him. "Aha, aha," he laughed. "Yeah, it was all Lakresha's idea. That conniving b'yatch."

Cedric stopped in his tracks. There was no way Junior would talk about Lakresha like that, even if she wasn't around, not unless he wanted to taste his own balls.

"You're not Junior," he said, his voice drenched with suspicion.

Larry took a few steps forwards, his axe still lowered. "Look, kid, cut me some slack, okay? I've been out of the game for a while, so why don't you just run, trip, and stagger along the ground for a bit so we can get the ball rolling?"

Cedric gasped. This wasn't Junior, or Freddy, or Bailey, or even *Jason*.

This was Larry 'Pigface' Travers, back from the dead, just like Junior said.

"Erm," Junior said, swallowing hard. He was too drunk to run with any real conviction. He had to think fast, to throw the maniac off his stride. "You do know I'm not black, don't you?"

The pig mask tilted. "I can *see* that," he said. "It's dark, but I'm not a complete buffoon." He raised the axe. He was close enough to swing, now. Close enough to slice the geek's face clean off.

Cedric knew that, too, and took a tentative step back. "After all these years of...of slicing and dicing...and you still don't know the rules?"

Again with the goddamn rules. *What is it with these kids?* What happened to the days when they saw you, realised you weren't spreading the word of the Lord, and ran the fuck away as fast as their little knobbly-kneed legs could carry them? "I don't have time for this, kid," Larry said. "Busy night ahead, and all that jazz."

Cedric held up a placatory hand. He could see three of them. It was ever so confusing. "No, you can't start killing white people until you've taken care of the black folk. You might as well just off the final girl first."

Larry sighed, lowered the axe once again. "Last time I listened to one of you whippersnappers, I ended up doing three minutes on gas-mark six." He nodded, knowingly. "No, I know what this is. You're just stalling for time, trying to save your own zit-peppered skin. Well, fool me once, shame on you, but fool me twice...yeah, I don't quite know how that's supposed to end." He'd never been very good with proverbs or adages. For the most part, they were utter bullshit.

Cedric, now trembling, said, "But if you're gonna do it right, it has to be in the correct order. Black folks, jocks, pretty girls, not-so-pretty girls, the nice guy, and then the final girl gets away. It's scripture, like the Bible and the Karma Sutra."

Larry frowned beneath the mask. "Strange that there was no mention of snotty-nosed geek-kids in there," he said.

Cedric cursed. He'd hoped Pigface hadn't noticed.

Why are you fucking around with this nincompoop? the mask said. *Swing, slash, dead...simple.*

"Now if we're talking about torture-porn—" Cedric said, but that was as far as he got. The flash of a blade distracted him, and then he fell silent, his words chopped perfectly in half by the axe. He tried to speak again, but nothing came out. He slowly reached up to straighten his glasses, but the lenses came away from the earpieces, which had been sliced entirely in half. The frames were sticky with something dark and viscous, and that was when he realised it was blood.

It was *his* blood.

"Why are you still standing?" Larry asked. And then the boy's face slipped down his skull and landed with a splat on the forest floor. The rest of him followed a second or two later. Staring down at the twitching, gargling, spitting, snot-bubble blowing body, Larry became acutely aware of the semi-erection in his slacks.

Talkative chap, wasn't he? the mask said. *He was right about killing the black people first, though.*

"Really?" Larry couldn't believe he'd fucked up already.

Nah, I'm just messing with you. You can kill 'em in whatever order you want to.

Larry sighed. "Good, because I'm done listening to their stupid rules. Where do they get off telling me when and who I can kill. *Ooooh, you can't kill me, I'm pregnant...oooh, I'm only seven, you can't kill me...ooooh, I'm a dog, and therefore out of bounds lest you piss off the animal-lovers.* It's ridiculous."

"Geeeeeergh," the faceless body said, sucking in air through what remained of its mouth and nose.

"Must be rusty," Larry said, raising the axe and bringing it down hard, embedding it between the eyes of the geek. Bones crunched, meat squelched, and a little fart trickled out of the boy's shorts. His legs stopped twitching almost immediately. Larry yanked the axe free and slung it across his shoulder. "Ah, it feels good to be back," he said. "I'll never forget the first time I sliced a teen's face off. It was in 1977. He was an ugly fucker, so in a way I did him a favour, but of course the *police* didn't see it that way." He began the unenviable task of dragging the body away from the main trail. Once he was deep enough into the woods, he left it slumped beside a tree and straightened up. His back audibly cracked, as did his knees, and something else that he couldn't quite put his finger on. "It feels like I've never been away," he said.

It smells like you've been in Guantanamo, the mask said.

"Gwantana-what?"

Never mind, fatso. Come on. Let's go kill some more adolescents.

"For the night is young!" Larry said, jollily.

Pity you're not, the mask muttered.

14
The Creek – 2014

Amanda must have worked her way through enough forest food to keep an African village alive for decades before she finally declared herself full. She'd attempted to get Freddy involved – *this one's perfectly safe, you just have to be careful of the spikes* or *you can only eat three of these at a time, four will kill you dead* – but he was having none of it. If he wouldn't eat the sprouts his mother put on his plate at home, there was little chance of him chowing down on leaves covered in unclassified faeces. Who knew what shit in the woods, apart from bears and popes. After watching Amanda pull bugs from her teeth for thirty minutes, he didn't think he'd ever eat again.

"So," she said, giving a tree a tight squeeze. It would have been a turn-on if he hadn't just watched her licking piss off a rock. "Are you looking forward to going back to college?"

Freddy glanced off into the middle-distance, though he didn't know why. He couldn't see squat. "Yes and no," he said. *Way to answer a question Cryptic Boy.*

"Ooooh, that sounds interesting," Amanda said, stroking a mushroom. It would have got any hot-under-the-collar juvenile excited, but again, Freddy felt nothing, not even the merest of stirrings. "Care to elaborate?"

"Don't get me wrong," he said. "I like college, but I just don't know where it's going to end. Most kids have plans; they already know what they want to do with their lives..."

"And you don't?"

He shrugged. "I always wanted to be a chef," he said, not knowing why he was telling her that. She didn't eat food unless it was covered in bugs, shit, or piss. "But I just don't think I could stand Gordon Ramsey shouting at me all the time."

Amanda laughed. "Silly," she said. "It wouldn't be all the time. He very seldom works weekends."

"Anyway, I've kind of given up on that idea. I'm leaning more toward a career in law."

"Wow. A lawyer." She whistled. Freddy dodged an errant bug as it flew from her mouth.

"No, I'm thinking of being one of those guards at the courthouse, the ones with the magic wands that beep for no reason."

Amanda's smile dropped, and then curled up again. "Well, it's a job. Somebody has to do it."

"So, what about you?" Freddy twisted his ankle on a pinecone, and then spent the rest of the next sentence pretending it hadn't hurt.

"I was thinking about doing entomology," she said. When Freddy frowned, she said, "It's the scientific study of insects."

"Ahhh," Freddy said. That was a terrible job for her. The temptation would always be there to nibble. After a few weeks she'd be the size of a houseboat and everyone would be wondering where the hell all the specimens were going. "I had you pegged more as a vet."

For a moment she looked offended. "Cats and dogs and all that malarkey?" she said. "No, I'm all for the preservation of

147

species, but pets are a completely different matter. In fact, everyone that keeps an animal as a pet should be taken out and shot with a twelve-bore shotgun."

Freddy decided not to mention Mr Tiggles and Rover waiting for him back at home. He didn't know how serious she really was about the whole mass execution thing.

"Animals shouldn't be dragged around on leads, put into cages no bigger than a coffin, fed other ground-up animals just to keep them alive. It's just not *natural*."

You know what else isn't natural? Freddy thought. *Eating bugs...*

"And don't even get me started on circuses."

"Okay, I won't," Freddy said. "So this entomology stuff? They do this at college?"

Amanda nodded. "Yeah, there's a whole course on it. You start off really small, like an ant or a money-spider, and work your way up. By the end of the term, I think we get to dissect a beetle."

"John, Ringo, Paul, or George?" Freddy chortled.

"We don't know their names," she said. "It's best not to get too close to something you're about to cut into hundreds of tiny pieces."

And on that note, Freddy thought, *I will never attempt another joke as long as I live...*

"I like you, Freddy," she said, so suddenly that it caught him off guard and he crashed into a tree, a tree that had every right to stand firm, since it had been there a helluva lot longer than he had.

"Excuse me?" he said, picking berries and twigs out of his hair.

Amanda sniggered. "I said I *like* you. You seem like a really nice guy, and even though your plans for the future involve frisking criminals just before they get sentenced to life-imprisonment, I really think you've got your head screwed on."

There was a compliment in there somewhere; Freddy just wished he had a microscope so he could find it. "I like you, too," he said. "Even though your favourite restaurant would be The Amazon, and you have a strange knack of whacking trees off without even noticing you're doing it."

Amanda moved toward him, slowly, staring down at her feet. Freddy stepped awkwardly from one foot to the other, anticipating her arrival. It seemed to take forever, and he had no fucking idea what to do with his hands. In the end he settled on shoving them as deep into his pockets as he could. They were safe in there. Sweaty, twitching, but safe.

Their faces were a foot apart when she said, "Kiss me."

Bugs, and shit, and piss, and bugs, and piss, and shit...they were all still in there, in that beautiful mouth he so badly wanted to brush with his own. He tried not to grimace as he moved in. This was everything he'd ever wanted; *she* was everything he'd ever wanted. He was damned if he was going to let a silly little thing like personal hygiene get in his way.

Then they were kissing, and it was wonderful. Freddy soon forgot about all the horrible things that had passed those lips only a few minutes before. The only thing passing them now was his tongue, which darted in and out of her mouth, like Kermit the Frog going down on Miss Piggy. *Lickit...lickit...lickit...*

Amanda pulled away first, but Freddy was glad to see that she was smiling. "You really know your way around the molars," she said. "Forget law. Maybe you should go into dentistry."

"Couldn't do it," Freddy said, crossing his legs to hide his erection. "Too much blood and spit for me."

Amanda reached down and took his hand. "Come on," she said. "The others will be wondering where we've got to."

"Probably think *Pigface* got us," Freddy said, laughing. He stopped, though, when he realised Amanda wasn't joining in. His no-joke policy hadn't lasted long. "Come on, then. Let's get back."

15

Camp Diamond Creek – 2014

Melissa and Bailey sat kissing on one sofa; Lakresha and Junior matched them tongue-for-tongue on the opposite sofa. And Jason, the camp counsellor, was considering grabbing his gorilla head from the closet, just so he didn't feel like a third wheel. The kissing was noisy, too, as if someone was unblocking a drain. Jason had had enough.

"Okay, guys, I'm gonna call it a night," he said, standing. He picked up his beer and walked across the room to the door. "I'll be over at the counsellor quarters if anyone needs anything." It looked as if they had everything they needed, though. It was as if they didn't even hear him. *I hope you run out of toilet roll, you bastards,* he thought as he stepped out into the night and closed the door quietly behind him.

It was a nice walk back to his own, private cabin, about a quarter of a mile from the main hub. His was the Ferrari of woodland residences, and the only one fitted with its own personal generator. He needed all the electricity he could muster to power his vast array of videogame consoles. There wasn't much else to do out there in the middle of nowhere; might as well kill some fucking aliens.

He almost collapsed onto his bunk; the walk and fresh air had made him dizzy. He didn't usually drink that much – there was never normally any booze around; it was all over at the new resort – and so it had hit him like a ten-ton-hammer. After watching the room spin for five minutes, he pushed up onto his elbows and, eventually, into a standing position.

"I'm coming to get you, Bowser," he said, slurring his words so badly, even *he* didn't know what he'd meant to say. He switched on the TV and his SNES (his favourite console of all time) and settled onto the edge of the bed.

There was something inherently wrong about being a moustachioed plumber whose only goal was to find and fuck the princess, even if it meant repeatedly battling a giant, spiky, fire-breathing turtle, but in that moment he couldn't quite put his finger on it. "Fucking love, man," Jason said. "True love."

He was halfway through level one when he realised someone was sitting next to him. Someone very big, and smelly; someone who shouldn't even *exist* anymore.

"That's what I'll never understand about you youngsters," Pigface said, shaking his head and snatching up the second controller. "Got the whole world out there, and you like to spend your days button-bashing in the dark."

Jason wanted to scream, but the vomit leaping up into his throat prevented him from doing so. No-one would have heard him, anyway, not at this time of night, not this far from the main cabin. He went to stand, but a giant hand came down on his thigh, holding him in place.

Pigface lifted a bloody finger to his lips. *Shhhhhhh.*

"You're *him*, aren't you? You're Larry Travers?" It came out all discombobulated, as if he was trying to speak a new language for the very first time. Of course, he wasn't. He'd been speaking English for almost eighteen years. It was the *fear* that made him sound half Polish, half German, and half Romany Gypsy.

Larry hadn't expected people to remember him, especially not one so young. It seemed that while he had been wasting his years in that ramshackle hut, his mother covering him in lotions and potions and trying to keep him on a leash, his legend had lived on. He didn't know whether to kill the kid or throw his arms around him.

"That's me," he said, firing up Luigi. The little green-coverall-wearing plumber ran alongside his brother, now. "I have no idea what I'm doing," Larry said as his character fell down a hole. "What is this thing, anyway? Some sort of sorcery?"

Jason had never been so utterly terrified in his entire life. "It's...it's a...super...Super Nintendo..." He was looking around for something he could use to protect himself from this maniac, but there was nothing in the vicinity. He did, however, see the bloody axe nestled between Pigface's knees, and that was the point his bowels decided to give up the ghost.

"Su-per Nin-ten-do," Larry said, punctuating each syllable as if they were altogether separate words. "Sounds *foreign*."

"Japanese," Jason said, squirming in his own mess. "Are you going to...*kill* me?" He'd rather not have broached the subject at all, but it was one of those things that had the potential to drive a person insane.

"*Japanese!*" Larry angrily said, dropping the controller as if it had electrocuted him. "*Japa-fuckin-ese!*"

Jason, suddenly free from Pigface's grasp, threw himself backwards. He'd intended a roll of sorts, but his feet caught in the controller cables and he ended up unable to move at all.

Then Pigface loomed over him, his breath rancid through the thin slit of a mouth-hole.

Tell me about it, said the mask.

"I might be *old*, son, but I still have what it takes." He lifted his hand, and Jason flinched, expecting to see the axe there.

But it wasn't the axe.

It was one of the console's controllers.

"Game over," Larry said, then forced the small, plastic thingamajig down as hard as he could. The boy screamed at just the right moment, which worked out quite nicely as far as Larry was concerned. Teeth shattered as the controller slammed into the boy's mouth. Down, down, down it went, and no matter how much the boy pushed back with his tongue, there was no stopping it.

When it was gone, when only the cable hung from the boy's wide-open and bloody maw, Larry took a step back to admire his handiwork. He'd never improvised so effectively before. Sure, there was that time he'd had to beat a girl to death with her own dildo, and that one occasion with the lawnmower in the communal gardens (whew, what a mess!) but this he was extremely proud of. They say you can't teach an old dog new tricks, and that was true...mostly. But Larry considered himself an artist, and artists never stop learning or striving to perfect their craft.

On the screen behind him, a little fat plumber wearing red coveralls was squashed by a giant spiky fire-breathing turtle.

"Kids," Larry said, picking up his axe and heading back into the night, where more joyous kills awaited him.

This was turning in to quite a remarkable comeback, even if he did say so himself.

16

Camp Diamond Creek – 2014

"Guys, we're going to take a little walk," Bailey said, hoisting Melissa up into his arms and carrying her across to the door. Junior lifted a hand to acknowledge the departing couple, but he was too busy sucking Lakresha's neck to offer them anything more.

"Have fun," Lakresha moaned, breathily.

"Oh, we *will*," Melissa said, pulling Bailey toward the door in a fit of excited giggles. Once they were gone, and the door firmly shut behind them, everything changed.

Lakresha climbed from Junior's lap and pushed his head away. "Git the fuck offa me," she said, wiping at her wet neck with the palm of her hand.

Junior wore the expression of a man who'd just been told he was, in fact, pregnant. Lakresha's arched eyebrows told him everything he needed to know. "You've got to be fucking *shitting* me," he said. "You were just trying to compete with Melissa and Bailey?"

"Since when do I ever let you nuzzle at my neck like that?" Lakresha said, her attitude a tangible, living thing. "Of course I was competing. Those fools thing they can out-fuck us. Well, I ain't playing. They want a war, they're going to fucking get one."

Just then the door flew open; Lakresha leapt onto Junior's lap and began to dry-hump him.

"Forgot my smokes," Bailey said, tiptoeing across the room and collecting them from the side of the sofa. He couldn't help notice how vigorous Lakresha was, how passionate and intense she was riding her man. He'd have to have words with Melissa, who needed to up her game. At the sound of the door closing, Lakresha climbed from Junior's lap.

"And *another* thing," she said, clicking her fingers. "When I'm *pretend*-fucking you, I expect a little eye-contact. Y'all be like looking around, as if you're chasing a moth or something."

Junior adjusted himself. His erection was vanishing quicker than a dude's self-esteem at a yoga class. "This is a little weird, even for you," he said. "Why y'all gotta be trying to keep up with the Joneses all of a sudden? They ain't no threat."

Taking a long, deep, controlled breath, Lakresha said, "It's not about keeping *up*."

Junior nodded.

"It's about leading the pack."

Junior sighed.

"I am a sexy motherfucker, and I ain't being outdone by a girl who paints her eyebrows on upside down." She stood and began pacing back and forth across the room. "You know what they're doing out there right now?"

"What I thought we would be doing in here?" Junior said.

"They're *screwing*, Junior. Screwing in the woods like a couple of feral bears."

"I had no idea that you felt like this," Junior said. She never told him *anything* until it was too late, and then he got the angry tirade version of it instead of the calm, *I-ain't-crazy* version. Sometimes he wondered why he put up with her shit, but then, that's what love was about, wasn't it? Taking abuse, being slapped, kicked, elbow-dropped, farted on, spat at, chewed on, with the occasional bout of unconsciousness? "So what do you want to do about it?"

Lakresha nodded. "Right, we need to make this place look like it's been hit by a bomb, like we've been fucking so hard that even the floorboards are all cracked and shit. Is there anything sperm-y we could flick about the place. Make it look like y'all exploded?"

"Couldn't we just go to bed?" Junior said. "You know, have some real, spontaneous sex?"

Lakresha tipped over the sofa closest to the door. "So we did it here. I was on top, knocked the sofa back six feet, eventually toppling it altogether." She smiled slightly. "Yeah, then we moved over here..." She waltzed across the room and picked up Freddy's guitar. Junior was about to tell her to put it down when she slammed it into the floor. Wooden splinters flew everywhere, shooting across the room like miniature arrows. The noise was horrible – like being in the front row at a Skrillex concert. "And we broke Freddy's guitar when you decided to see if it fitted up in me."

"Are you *insane*!" Junior gasped. "That was his pride and joy. Why the hell would I try to *fuck* you with it?"

"Because we're crazy and sexy!" Lakresha said, almost growled. She had the same look a puma gets just before leaping on a moose's back and sinking its teeth in.

Dropping the decimated instrument, she walked over to Junior and slapped him once, hard, across the face. His head jerked to the side, and when it came back, it wore the same expression as a moose when it realises it's about to get royally fucked up by a puma. "Woman, are you outta your damn mind?"

She grabbed his head and pulled him in for a long, intense, and rather violent kiss. Junior didn't know whether to rejoice or call an ambulance.

She pulled away. "They've got *nothing* on us," she said, chewing his lip as if it were a piece of a raw meat. Junior groaned. From seemingly nowhere, Lakresha produced a set of handcuffs. Now Junior, who was horny as hell, would have normally jumped at the chance of a little kinky play, but with Lakresha the way she currently was – savage, determined, and a little bit mental – he didn't fancy his chances.

"Whatcha gonna do with *those*?" Junior said, a little scared.

She slapped one of the cuffs down on his wrist, and the other on her own. "We're gonna play convicts," she said. "*Sex* convicts. I want them to find us like this when they get back, bound together, naked and sweaty, looking like we both just got fucked by the entire population of B-wing."

"But we're not actually gonna *do* anything?" Junior was perplexed. This was the worst role-playing he'd ever done.

"No, but we want *them* to think we've done shit." She smiled, nodding, as if her genius plan was so good, it deserved noddings and smilings.

Junior looked down at the cuffs and tried to work out how they were going to be naked when Bailey and Melissa returned. He'd have to slip his tee-shirt off, slide it over the chain to Lakresha's side and the...well then *she* would be wearing it.

Bailey and Melissa would return to find Junior dressed in Lakresha's clothes, and Lakresha in Junior's. If that didn't make them realise they couldn't out-freak the black folks, nothing would.

"Can I ask you something?" Junior said.

"You just did," Lakresha replied, trying to take off her halter-neck with one hand.

"Can I ask you a *second* question, then?"

"You can ask me a third." The strap was almost over her head now. Just a little bit further...

"Do you have the keys for these cuffs?"

She stopped yanking and tugging at her dress and froze, as if she'd accidentally caught the eye of Medusa. Then she shook her head and went back to removing her clothes. "We'll cross that bridge when we come to it," she said. "Get your trousers down, and grab a hold of my bra, if you can."

Junior made a mental note to finish the relationship as soon as they got back to the real world.

17

A Bit of Dirty Ground in the Woods – 2014

Bailey pushed himself as deep as he could go, but the amount of drink he'd imbibed coupled with the cheese he'd smoked had left him practically impotent. It was like throwing a rubber band at a very hairy vagina; there was no simile for her lady-parts.

"Whoa," Bailey said, snorting. "I was almost in that time."

Melissa patted him on the back and sighed. How long had they been at it? She didn't know, but things were taking root around her, and possibly inside her. The leaves above were green when they started, but now they were browning and falling, or perhaps that was just her imagination. Either way, Bailey was about as useful as a pair of tits on a fish tonight. She'd give him five more minutes of fumbling before telling him to get off. She was sore downstairs, but that wasn't anything to do with him. She'd seen the thorns when she lay down.

"Maybe it's you," Bailey said, taking aim once again. He closed one eye, as if that would make any difference, and then poked her in the knee with his rubber-band penis. He couldn't have been further away if he'd been fucking her via Skype.

"It's not *me*," Melissa said. "It's all that shit you've been smoking." She shook her head, looking positively dejected. She knew what Junior and Lakresha were doing back at the cabin. *I bet he's giving it to her good. I bet she's screaming, and they're both sweating and covered in spit and piss and whatever else they're into.*

"I've just cum," she lied. Bailey was too stupid to know that when a woman said it in the past tense, they'd faked it.

"Awesome," Bailey said, rolling onto his back. "And this time I didn't even have to put it in. Shit I'm good!"

Melissa stretched, arching her back, scraping the ant-farm from her ass cheeks. "Yeah, you're a regular John Holmes," she said. "Do you remember where I put my panties?" She raked around in the dark, trying to find the pink briefs she'd foolishly torn off many moons ago, or so it seemed.

Bailey lit a cigarette and, blowing a plume of blue smoke into the night, said, "I should be a porn star. I mean, I've got a great body, and my dick's awesome when it's on form."

"Go for it," Melissa said, impetuously. She was too busy looking for her panties. *Didn't I hang them on the branch with my shorts?* Obviously not, for they weren't there now. Maybe they had been stolen by an aroused bat. Who knew what creatures were out there in the woods, watching, waiting, masturbating...

"Yeah, I'd be one of those guys that fucked midgets, even though they're, like, small, and stuff, but they really like to fuck. Did you hear about how Judy Garland got gangbanged making that wizard film of hers?"

Melissa stood. Where the *fuck* were her knickers? "I don't think that happened," she said. "Maybe you're confusing her with Liza Minelli. I know she has a fetish for weird small guys that look as if they live in a world of their own."

A horrific *soueeeeee* tore through the night. Melissa forgot all about her panties and climbed into her shorts. "What the hell was that?" she gasped, scanning the darkness.

"Sounded like *soueeeeee*," Bailey said, prodding at his uber-flaccid penis as if he was discovering it for the very first time.

Melissa pulled her top on. "Yeah, but what goes *soueeeee*?"

"You did, just," Bailey said. "Have you ever looked at a penis and thought, wow, that's a really odd-looking piece of meat?"

Melissa wasn't interested. "Bailey, there's something out there, something going *soueeeee*." She worked her way through all the wild animals she knew (it didn't take too long) and came to the conclusion that she had no idea what went *soueeeee*.

There it was again, only this time much closer. So close, she heard the cough that followed it.

"Seriously, Bailey," she said. "Did you hear that? It went *soueeeee-cough-cough*. What goes *soueeeee-cough-cough*?"

"You did, just," Bailey said, giving his member a little flick, like a child taunting a worm.

"For fuck's sake!" a voice said, a voice that was soon accompanied by a body, a body that stepped out from behind a tree. It wore a beautifully-ironed white apron, spattered here and there with something much darker. The pig mask the figure wore would have been laughable if it wasn't so damn terrifying. In its right hand was an axe. It was the kind of axe that people only used for chopping up other people. "Pigs go *soueeeee*," it said. "Don't you kids know anything?"

Melissa was paralysed with fear, which was a shame because now would have been a great time to start running. On the forest floor, Bailey rolled around, trying to get to his feet, but he was so stoned and drunk that he'd have had more chance attaining an erection than standing up.

No, Melissa thought. *This is some kind of joke. Another one of Jason's silly costumes.* Well, it was a joke she didn't find funny. "You might have been able to scare Amanda," she said to the costumed interloper, "but you're fucking with the wrong girl by taking me on, Jason."

Pigface snorted, shaking his head. "Why does everyone keep getting me mixed up?" he said. "What's a guy got to do to get some recognition around here? I'm not fucking Jason. That would be a stupid name for a slasher maniac. I'm Larry 'Pigface' Travers, and your recent bout of sexing has put you next on my list of people to brutally murder." He put his hand behind his back and then, as if by magic, came out with Melissa's missing panties. He sniffed them, snorted them as if trying to locate truffles, and said, "I'm so glad neither of you are running. I'm not as young as I used to be. Not sure my ticker could take a high-speed pursuit through the trees."

As if Pigface had reminded her of something extremely important, Melissa turned and ran. It was an odd run, not nearly as controlled as she'd hoped. It was how one might run through a field of invisible landmines, but Melissa didn't care. What mattered was that she was running away from the axe-wielding maniac. It came, therefore, as quite a shock when she found herself back where she'd started.

"Get lost, did we?" Pigface said. "I know. Bloody trees all look the same."

"Please don't kill us!" she cried, helping Bailey to his feet and putting him between herself and Pigface. It seemed like the right thing to do. "My father is an extremely wealthy man. If, say, you were to kidnap us instead, he would pay you a handsome sum just to get me back." She didn't know whether bartering was the correct angle to go for, but she was desperate, and it was true — her father had more money than Scrooge McDuck, and swam in it like Scrooge, too.

"I'm not much of a kidnapper," Larry said, scratching his snout with the blade of the axe. "No, it takes a special kind of lunatic to be in that game. I'm more of a hack and slash kind of fella. Don't have much use for money where I come from. My mom pays the milkman in advance, and I don't think she uses cash."

Bailey took a step toward Larry, holding his fists up like one of those boxers from the days when everything was in black-and-white. "I'm afraid I'm not going to let you hurt my woman," he said, dropping into some weird stance that made him look as if he was about to take a dump. "Why don't you put the axe down and we can settle this—"

Larry threw the axe at the boy, watched as it went handle over blade over handle in what appeared to be super slow-motion. Eventually it slammed into the boy's chest, knocking him back several metres.

"*Squeeee!*" Larry said.

"Who throws an axe?" Bailey grunted, tentatively fingering the wooden handle jutting from his torso. Warm, sticky blood began to drip down his body, slipping into his muscular abs. If he hadn't been so stoned, it would have hurt like a sonofabitch.

Melissa screamed as Bailey turned to her, almost clonking her in the face with the protruding handle. His penis had fully retracted into him and it had taken his balls with it. She did the only thing she could.

She turned and ran.

When she arrived back at the same spot a few moments later, the killer had already pulled the axe from Bailey's chest and decapitated him. "Ah, took a wrong turn again, did we?" Larry said, kicking Bailey's severed head as hard as he could into the darkness. "You know, Hansel and Gretel had the right idea, but I don't suppose you thought to bring breadcrumbs."

"Why are you *doing* this?" Melissa sobbed. "What did we ever do to *you*?"

Larry tilted his head as he considered the question. "Well," he said. "For *one*, you're here in Diamond Creek. And two...I guess there isn't a two."

Melissa thought about the story Jason had told them earlier, about how Larry Travers had been bullied. That was why he'd taken up the axe and started killing innocent teens. As far as motives went, it was pretty thin, but it was better than just randomly killing people, like that Zodiac guy, or George W. Bush.

"I was bullied too," Melissa said.

"No you weren't," Larry replied.

"Was *too*."

"Was *not*."

"Well, a girl once trod on my foot, and I don't think it was an accident."

"Did she say sorry?"

Melissa nodded.

"Then it was an accident."

Shit! He's gonna kill me. He's gonna kill me and I'm going to be all over the news, and when they find me, I won't be wearing any panties.

"I'm the final girl," Melissa lied. "You can't kill me. Don't you know about the *rules?*"

Larry *soueeeeed* and limped toward Melissa, axe raised. He would have run – or at least tried to – but one of his worms had popped out for a little look around and he didn't want to hurt it. He swung the axe in a wide arc. It made a wonderful noise as it sliced through the air – a whoosh that would have made Zorro jealous – and an even better noise when it thumped into the girl's neck.

Her scream was cut off at almost the exact same time as her head; Larry didn't know whether that was science, or just a coincidence. The head rolled one way, the body fell the other, and Larry *squeeed* triumphantly, watching as the blood continued to pump from the stump of the girl's neck.

If she'd turned left instead of right, the mask said, *she'd have probably got away.*

"Yeah, and if I wore a gown and collar and called myself father, I'd be a paedophile," Larry said. He wasn't interested in what the mask had to say. If indeed it was saying anything at all.

I'm just saying, if she'd run the right way, you wouldn't have caught her. You're an old man, out of your comfort zone. Maybe your mother's right. You should start knitting.

"Maybe she was right about *one* thing," Larry said. "That you should be *discarded* of. You've done nothing but whine since I put you on. Honestly, you're like a twelve year-old goth chick."

The mask fell silent. There was no point in arguing; it wouldn't get either of them anywhere. Larry was more stubborn than a shit-stain in a white mohair rug.

18
Jason's Cabin – 2014

Amanda saw it first. Freddy saw it second, which wasn't much to be proud of since he was only one of two. A small cabin, its door wide open. Through the window something glimmered, as if the occupant was watching TV. In which case, why was the door swinging on its hinges? Had the tenant popped out for a moment? Perhaps they had TV, but nowhere to put their number twos.

"I thought we were the only ones up here," Freddy said as they approached the cabin. At the first sign of a) gingerbread or b) a witch, he was getting the hell out of there.

Amanda let go of Freddy's hand and picked up a stick. She didn't know why, but it seemed better to have one than not to have one. "Something's not right," she said. As if to punctuate her sentence, the door slammed back against the cabin before flying wide again. She wouldn't have minded, but the wind didn't seem strong enough for all that nonsense.

"Are we going to poke something?" Freddy asked, gesturing to the stick she now wielded.

"Not if we don't have to," she said. "Have you ever been in a fight before?"

Freddy frowned. What kind of a question was that? "Depends what you call a fight," he said. "My little sister once kicked me in the nuts, and I made this awfully plaintive sound as I slid down the doorframe."

"Have you ever punched a person?"

"I've punched a doorframe."

"You'd better get behind me," Amanda said, raising the stick. "If this gets ugly, I'm the one with the stick." *And apparently the balls*, she thought but didn't add.

They were pressed up against the cabin, the door swinging raucously to their left. Amanda was holding the stick as if it were a gun; her finger even rested on an invisible trigger. *This*, Freddy thought, *is not going to end well.*

Amanda took a deep breath and waited for the door to swing open again. When it did...well, she missed it and had to wait for the next one. Freddy thought they would be out there all night, squashed up against the mystery cabin as if they were CSI: Diamond Creek. After another minute, Amanda lunged for the open door, and whatever she saw inside drained her of all colour in an instant.

"What?" Freddy whispered. "What is it?"

She brought her hand up to her mouth, which had fallen open into a perpetual O. "Jason," she whispered. "It's Jason."

Freddy straightened up. It was another one of Jason's tricks. Well, Freddy wasn't in the mood for it. He marched past Amanda and into the cabin.

"Come on, you British bastard," he said to the body on the bed. "Get your ass up so I can kick or punch it. You've frightened my girl for the second time, and I'm about to teach you some darned manners." He went to roll his sleeves up, which was no good since he was wearing a tee-shirt.

The TV showed Mario running through some tunnel or other and coming out in an entirely different world. Unless Jason was a master of videogames, and able to play without looking at the screen, Freddy figured it was running on demo.

"Quit playing around, freak," Freddy said, giving the cable hanging out of Jason's mouth a good yank. It took more force than he'd expected because on the end of that cable was a games controller, the kind that should in no way, shape, or form, fit down someone's throat. The fact that it was covered in blood and viscera was not lost on Freddy.

"Oh my god!" Amanda said. At some point she'd snuck up on Freddy and was now right behind him, staring down at the body on the bed. "Is he...is he *dead*?"

Now Freddy was no expert. He'd once seen a dead cat, but that one's eyes had been popped out along with the majority of its innards, so it had been easy to make an assessment. He'd never seen a dead human before, so he wasn't quite sure what one would look like, but if there was an entry in the dictionary (*Dead human: Noun. A person that isn't likely to be doing the Macarena any time soon, or much else, for that matter*) he was almost certain there would be a picture of Jason the camp counsellor next to it.

He dropped the videogame controller and wiped his hands on his tee-shirt. "Shit! He is! He's dead!" But that couldn't be right, could it? He was back at the main cabin with the others, or had been when he and Amanda had left. Somewhere along the line, the shit had hit the fan.

Amanda grabbed onto Freddy's arm and squeezed tight. So tight, in fact, that Freddy made hissings and whimperings. "Who *did* this to him?" she said, suddenly very aware that she was holding a stick, and not a very big one at that.

"I don't know," Freddy said, wishing he had picked up a stick when Amanda did. "Maybe he did it to *himself*?" The fact that there was a question-mark at the end of his sentence told him how ridiculous that was.

"What? He decided to off himself in the middle of a game, and the best way to do that was to ram that thing" – she pointed to the blood-drenched controller – "down his own throat until he choked to death?"

"Look, we can hypothesise later. We need to get back to the others. There's a maniac out there, and if you hadn't noticed, we're hardly equipped to deal with one."

Amanda nodded, but there was something Freddy hadn't considered and she needed to put it out there before they started back for the cabin. "Think about this for a moment," she said. "When we left, Jason was at the cabin. Right?"

Freddy said, "Right," but he had no idea where she was going with it.

"And now he's here. Deader than a dodo at a disco. Correct?"

"Have you ever thought about giving entomology a miss and going straight for the FBI?"

Amanda held both hands out. The stick dropped to the floorboards. It didn't matter, though, as no matter how hard or repeatedly you poked a maniac, it wouldn't make a blind bit of difference. "What if one of *us* killed him?"

"But we were together the whole time," Freddy said, somewhat defensively, and more than a little stupidly.

"Not *us*," Amanda said. "One of our *group*."

That, Freddy thought, made more sense. "Ah," he said. "But why?"

Amanda shrugged. "We don't know what happened once we left. Jason could have pissed one of them off." Or all of them. Shit, what if they were all in on it, like in that film with the fisherman and Jennifer Love Hewitt? The thought sent a shiver down her spine.

"I bet it was Bailey," Freddy surmised. "That guy's done more 'roids than Carrot Top."

"If it *was* Bailey," Amanda said, "then Melissa's in on it, too. And if Melissa was in on it, Lakresha *knows* about it. And if Lakresha knows about it, she's already slapped Junior upside the head and warned him not to tell." God, it was a nightmare. An actual living nightmare, and they'd been dropped feet-first into it.

"We need to call the cops," Freddy said. "Do you have your phone?"

Amanda shook her head. "It's back at the cabin, but I couldn't get a signal earlier anyway. It had less bars than Abu Dhabi." She gripped even tighter onto Freddy's arm, causing him to make a sound he hadn't heard since the first time he'd successfully masturbated. "I'm scared, Freddy," she said.

Prising her hand from his recessed flesh, Freddy turned to face her. "We're going to be okay," he said. "We just need to stick together. We can't go back to the cabin. It's too dangerous. I say we head over to the new resort. Jason said it was only a mile away. We can make it in fifteen minutes if we walk fast."

Amanda took a deep breath. Freddy was right. They needed to get as far away from Camp Diamond Creek as they could, at least for the time being. The new resort would have a telephone, security-guards, counsellors, and people in general walking around the place. They would be safe there until they figured out what was going on.

"You okay?" Freddy said, taking her by the shoulders and staring deep into her watery, hazel eyes. She nodded, forced a smile. Freddy reached up and fingered one of her dimples. "Not as deep as they look," he said, probing around with his *digitus medius*. "Come on. Let's get the hell out of here."

Outside it had started to rain, which was fine. It's when you're inside and it rains that something's very wrong. They took off at a brisk pace, and were doing reasonably well until Amanda pulled up. Her hand slipped from Freddy's, who didn't seem to realise it for another ten feet or so.

"What?" he said when he finally realised Amanda was no longer at his side, or in his hand.

"He said it was a mile from here," said Amanda. "Did he mention which direction that was in?"

"Yeah, he said...well...I'm pretty sure he said it was...*FUCK*!"

"For all we know it's a mile up," Amanda said. "We could guess, I suppose, but if you take into account the possible basic directions of north, south, east, and west, that would leave us a twenty-five percent chance of landing at the new resort. Then there are your variables: north-east, north-west, south-west, east-west..."

"I'm not sure you can count east-west," Freddy said. "And we've been hanging around with Cedric for far too long."

"We have no choice but to keep walking," Amanda said, "and hope that we hit this fabled resort in the dark with no idea of where we're going."

"Out here, where every tree looks the same and every branch looks like it's designed to kill or severely maim us, what could possibly go wrong?"

19
Camp Diamond Creek – 2014

"It's no use," Junior said, gasping for breath. "We're just going to have to stay like this."

They had been trying to get naked for thirty minutes, and had succeeded as best as they could, though the cuff chain was now swamped with clothes. If they were to stretch out, Lakresha and Junior would look like the world's strangest washing line.

"*Fuckit!*" Lakresha said, pulling Junior across the room and slumping onto the couch. He followed suit, not that he had much choice in the matter. "Now we just have to wait."

The room was in all sorts of disarray. Cushions had been removed from chairs; anything tall enough to be toppled *had* been toppled, and a thick coating of silly-string made it look like the scene of some wild clown orgy. Junior had no idea where she'd got the silly string from; he was just glad there weren't strands of it hanging out of his person.

"If this doesn't make them realise they're fucking with the wrong freaks," Lakresha said, scrutinising their surroundings, "then I don't know what will."

"Oh, we're *definitely* going to look like freaks," Junior said, pulling a guitar string from his ass cheeks. It wasn't the G, which would have made for a decent joke.

"Y'all think I'm crazy?" Lakresha said, in a tone that suggested he'd better consider his answer carefully and then tell her the opposite.

"No," he said.

"Would that be your answer if we weren't cuffed together?"

"*Hell* no."

Lakresha sighed. Perhaps things *had* gone a little too far. What was it they said about love? *When love is not madness, it is not love?* Lakresha had no idea where she'd heard that before – it was probably from a Dr Dre song – but sitting there, sweaty and naked, surrounded by broken shit and waiting for an inferior couple to return, it kind of made perfect sense.

"Junior?"

Junior was exhausted and simply wanted bed, preferably alone. "Hm?"

"What's that flashing red light in the corner?"

Without opening his eyes, Junior said, "Could it be a flashing red light?"

Lakresha nudged him with her elbow until he opened his eyes. "I'm serious. What is it?"

Junior saw it, too; an intermittently flickering red light, small enough to go unnoticed if, indeed, you weren't looking for it. "Maybe it's the smoke alarm," he said, yawning. "I'd take the battery out, but you'd have to come with me."

"It's not a smoke alarm," Lakresha said. "Bailey's been smoking all night long."

"Maybe it's one of those silent ones," Junior said, not knowing if such things existed and not caring in the slightest. "Can we just go to bed?"

Lakresha shook her head. She had a very bad feeling about the flashing light. A very, very bad feeling.

"Get yo ass up," she said, standing. Junior wasn't so enthusiastic. "Junior, I'm not fuckin' around."

"Alright, alright, I'm up," Junior said, even though he wasn't, not quite. All of a sudden he felt very vulnerable. Being naked (in a fashion) and handcuffed (definitely) had that effect on some people. "It's a flashing red light, that's all."

"People don't just *have* flashing red lights," Lakresha said, yanking Junior to his feet. "They usually mean something, or go somewhere, or do something, otherwise what's the point?"

They moved slowly across the room, dodging broken furniture and picking up silly string between their toes. Junior trod on a piece of Lego and, after a few seconds of absolute agony, tried to figure out where it had come from. But that was the thing about Lego; you didn't have to own any to find yourself stepping on it. It was as if it came from an alternate dimension, its only purpose to cause as much pain as possible.

Lakresha glanced up at the source of the flashing light; a small black box fitted with a lens and, well, a flashing red light. It was Sellotaped to the ceiling right in the corner.

"See," Junior said. "It's just a small black box fitted with a lens and a flashing red light, Sellotaped to the ceiling." He yawned again. "Can we go to bed now? We've got a lot of tidying up to do in the morning."

"It's a *camera!*" Lakresha gasped. "Junior, it's a fucking *camera*. Why would there be a camera in here?"

"It's *not* a camera," Junior said, but now that she mentioned it...it did look suspiciously like a camera. "Okay, maybe it *is* a camera, but I doubt it's working."

"It's got a flashing red light," Lakresha said, covering her nipples with one hand and her lady-bush with the other. "It's a working *camera*, and it's been watching us this entire time."

"We don't know that," Junior said, pulling a tartan sock over his schlong.

"What if people can see us right now? What if this whole night has been live streaming to the fucking new resort? What if we're on a BIG FUCKING SCREEN RIGHT NOW!?"

"Okay, sweetie, you need to calm the *fuck* down." But what if she was right?

What if the whole thing had been caught on camera? Out of context, the last hour would have come across as a little bizarre. It didn't make much sense *in* context, either. "Okay, maybe we should move to a different room. I'm wearing a sock on my cock and all of a sudden I don't feel—"

Just then, the window at the back of the room exploded. Lakresha screamed and instinctively tossed herself to the ground, but Junior remained on his feet, which left Lakresha dangling from his arm like some novelty bracelet.

The ball rolled to a stop an inch from Lakresha's horrified face, only it wasn't a ball at all. It had a nose, and eyes, and ears, and all of it looked familiar. She screamed again, and then a third time, just in case the previous two weren't quite good enough.

"HOLY SHIT!" Junior screamed, staring down at the severed head. "IT'S FUCKING BAILEY!"

"*Where's the rest of him*!?" Lakresha screeched, so shrilly that eight miles away, in a small village called Burton, a German Shepherd's ears pricked up.

Junior helped Lakresha to her feet, completely unaware that his sock had fallen off. "Is he dead!?" Junior said, nudging the head with his bare foot.

Lakresha rolled her eyes. "No. He just needs a good doctor." She shook her head. "Of *course* he's fucking dead! But who did the dead-ing?" She turned her attention to the shattered window. Someone was out there. Someone had to have thrown the head. Someone had to have killed...

"You don't think Melissa did this, do you?" Junior said. "I mean, to try to out-freak us?"

"I wouldn't put it past her," Lakresha said. That bitch would do anything to outdo her, and nothing said freaky quite like the decapitation of one's fuck-buddy.

A moment later a second head came through the window. This one landed a few inches from Bailey's; even though its eyes had been gouged out, Lakresha could see exactly who it was. "Okay, well that rules out Melissa," she said. "Why are we just standing here? Shouldn't we be running, or something to that effect?"

"That's the sanest thing you've said all night," Junior said, lunging for the door. The axe blade came through at just the right moment – though not for Junior, who lost three fingers in an instant.

Lakresha screamed. That dog eight miles away started chasing its tail. Junior fell to the floor, dragging Lakresha with him. His knuckle-stumps spurted blood everywhere. He picked up one severed finger and balanced it back on his hand, where it stood for less than a second before toppling off again.

The heel of the axe penetrated the door again, and again, and...well, you get the idea. Splinters rained down on the cowering couple. It wouldn't have been so bad, but the door was unlocked.

"Get up, Junior!" Lakresha screamed. The dog over in Burton had had enough and went for a little lie down.

Junior dropped the fingers he'd collected and scrambled back a few feet, just in time to see the axe smash a hole in the top half of the door. Just in time to see the dirty, pink snout push through it.

"Heeeeeeeeere's Larry!" Pigface said, though he felt stupid the moment the words passed his lips. That wasn't the kind of thing an axe-wielding lunatic would say. Perhaps in some Hollywood horror film, but even *then...*

"It's the pig guy!" Lakresha said. She'd given up trying to get Junior to stand, and was now dragging him across the floor like a recalcitrant puppy. The legend was true. The bullied kid had returned, and now he had a couple of handcuffed, naked, black folk at his disposal. The only way they could have made it any easier for him was if they'd started to chop *themselves* up.

The door gently pushed open. "Oh," Pigface said, checking the latch. "Why didn't you tell me it was open? Could have saved me a lot of swinging. I'm not as young as I used to be, you know."

"Please don't kill us!" Lakresha said. There was no way out, except past Pigface, and Junior was in no condition to make a run for it. He was in shock, too busy drooling and counting his missing fingers.

Using his axe as a walking-stick, Pigface limped into the cabin, and even though it was a wholly different cabin than the one he'd almost died in back in '78, a tingle ran along his spine and a little trickle of urine warmed his leg.

Are you going to cry? the mask asked. *Because if you are, I'd rather you took me off first.*

"I'm not going to fucking cry," Pigface said, perusing his surroundings and catching his breath.

"Of course you're not," Lakresha said. "Who said you *were*?" She'd seen enough movies to know that the best way to get out of a sticky situation was to empathise with the maniac. She'd also seen loads of films where the heroine takes it a step further and tries to seduce her would-be attacker. She drew the line at that.

Things have changed. Haven't they, Larry? the mask said, almost hissed.

"*Nothing's* changed," Pigface replied.

"Well, Junior only has a finger and a thumb now," Lakresha said. "If y'all don't call that a difference, I don't know what is."

She thinks you're talking to her, the mask said. *How funny!*

"I'm not talking to you," Pigface told the cowering girl. His arm was aching from attacking the door, and so it took a lot of effort just to get the axe up in the air. "Just before I kill you," he said, frowning. "I need to know one thing."

"Shoot," Lakresha said, "and then reconsider the killing part of that sentence."

"Why are you naked and handcuffed together?"

Lakresha sighed. "It's a long story," she said. "And if you're going to kill us anyway, I'm going to take it to the grave."

Pigface raised the axe higher. *God, I must have pulled something*, he thought, wincing as bolts of sharp pain surged through his tendons. "Suit yourself," he said. "But remember...this is how they'll find you."

And with that he started hacking away.

And Lakresha's piercing – yet inaudible to the human ear – screams slowly sent that poor German Shepherd, so many miles away, insane.

20
Woods! Lots of Woods! – 2014

There were trees. *Lots* of trees. So many trees that neither Freddy nor Amanda could see the woods for them. It was also very dark, which made seeing *all* of the trees that little bit more difficult, which was why they both sported bruises and grazes and various other tree-related wounds.

"I think we're lost," Freddy said. He was sore and bereft of breath; being lost was the last thing they needed.

"I'm not sure lost is the right word for what we are," Amanda said, taking a breather against a tree, of which there were many, but you already knew that.

"Buggered?" Freddy said. "Hopeless? Desperate? Knackered? Fucked?"

"Not to mention forlorn, exhausted, and clichéd," Amanda said. "On the bright side..." She trailed off, realising there really wasn't one.

"We're going to get out of this alive," Freddy said. "We can't be far from the new resort. We must have walked a mile by now."

"If we were facing the wrong way to start with, we're now a mile and a half *away* from it." Amanda straightened up and sighed. "How many hours until sun-up?"

Freddy checked the space on his wrist where a watch would have been, if people still wore watches in the age of cell-phones. "I'd say quite a few." It was a rough estimate, but you work with what you have.

"Well, at least we won't starve out here," Amanda said, picking up a muddy leaf and nibbling at it like the very, *very* hungry caterpillar.

You *won't*, Freddy thought, fighting down the bile. He couldn't eat what she was eating, no matter how much his stomach complained. Therefore he would die, and Amanda would wait a few hours – she wasn't a *complete* animal – before whipping up a quick fire and toasting his meatiest parts over it.

Freddy crossed his legs, and said, "You're not going to *eat* me, are you?"

She frowned, then laughed, then frowned again. "Not *right* away," she said. "I mean, I like you, but I think we should get to know each other a little first. Maybe light a few candles, have a nice bubble-bath, give it a good wash and I'll think about it."

It was Freddy's turn to do the frowning. Then it made sense, and embarrassment washed over him. "You're talking about oral sex?" he said. "No, I meant actually *eat* me. Like those rugby players in the Andes?"

"I didn't eat *any* rugby players in the Andes," Amanda said. "And besides, I'm vegetarian."

"But the bugs?" Freddy said, with no small amount of confusion.

"Bugs aren't *meat*," she said, shaking her head and rolling her eyes and performing many other patronising gestures. "Loads of protein in a bug, though."

"So you're not one of those veggies that refuses to eat anything with a face?" Freddy said. "I'm assuming insects have faces?" Unlike Amanda, he wasn't about to take a course in entomology. She'd probably already seen one under a microscope, and therefore had the upper hand.

"I'm one of those veggies that pretends to be all uppity about things, but if it came down to it, I'd eat a scabby horse between two pieces of pig."

Freddy nodded. He knew that type. Not nearly as bad as the ones that don't count fish as meat, though. He'd once known a vegetarian who only ate chicken because they were descendants of dinosaurs, and therefore as good as extinct.

They walked for another quarter of a mile, though neither of them knew that, before arriving at a mesh fence. It must have been twelve feet high, and the mesh was that small stuff you couldn't get your feet into, even if you were a hobbit. On the other side of the fence was, unsurprisingly, more trees.

"What now?" Amanda said, testing the mesh for sturdiness.

"This isn't terrible news," Freddy said, a little more excitedly than he'd intended. "Fences like this aren't just put there for show. They're to keep things out...or in, depending on which side of the fence you're on."

"Are we in?" Amanda said.

"To anyone outside, I'd say so." Freddy was losing his train of thought. "Anyway, if we follow this fence all the way around, eventually we're going to come to the exit, or the entrance, depending on which way you're going."

Amanda's eyes lit up. "You're not as dumb as you look," she said. Freddy took it as a compliment, proving that she was sorely mistaken. "So which way do we go?" Since it was a fence, it ran in two directions. That way and the other way. One would, without doubt, be closer to the exit than the other, and so you could guarantee that they would opt for the other.

"I don't think it matters," Freddy said. "Let's just walk, see where it gets us."

Amanda smiled. "And if I get hungry, I can always eat you."

Freddy sniggered, but it was a nervous snigger. "Yeah," he said. *Please don't*, he thought.

21
Woods! But Not as Many as the Last Chapter – 2014

Larry was getting fed up of walking. If there was one thing he hated more than horny teenagers getting stoned and having intercourse with anything that wasn't nailed down, it was walking for the sake of walking. At least with running, you got it over with, and with minimal fuss. A-to-B in half the time it would take you to walk it. *If only*, Larry thought, *I could still run.* He'd have covered twice as much ground by now.

It didn't matter. He *couldn't* run. Hadn't tried for more than thirty years, and wasn't about to tonight. His hips were grinding in their sockets as it was, and he had a feeling his ticker wouldn't take a sudden burst of energy (and it would have been very sudden, and very, very short, not dissimilar to the heart-attack he would suffer if he took it up a notch).

Maybe you got 'em all, the mask said. *I mean, the camp's not as nice as it used to be. Maybe that's yer lot...*

Larry, breathless and drained, leaned against a tree. Had his axe always been so cumbersome? So damn heavy? Maybe it was time to switch to something lighter, something that didn't leave his arm dangling listlessly from its socket. How heavy was a garrotte?

"I don't think I got them *all*," Larry huffed. "It wouldn't make sense."

I don't follow.

"Well, if you didn't notice, the two I just butchered were of the...well, they were *black*."

I did notice. You're not about to go all New Century Foundation on me, are you?

"I have no idea what that is," Larry said. "What I'm trying to say is that, if the rules still apply, they *can't* be the last."

Sounds a bit racist to me, Larry, the mask said, tutting. *It comes to something, in this day and age, when even your psycho-killer sounds like Mel Gibson at a KKK garden party.*

Larry sighed. "I'm not racist at all," he said. "If anything, I kill more *white* people than black."

Reverse racism! the mask said. *I don't know how you sleep at night!*

"Well, once ma's finished with her saucy book and the smelly pillar candle, pretty well, actually." He shuddered and pushed the image from his mind. "What I'm trying to get at, and I'm not racist at all—"

Exactly what a racist would say—

"—is that those cuffed kids – which was a little odd, wasn't it? – were black, and that everyone knows that the final girl has to be white, *ergo*—"

There's nothing more racist than Latin, the mask said.

"*Ergo*," Larry said, louder. "The final girl is still out there, somewhere, running through the trees probably. She'll be tripping up on absolutely nothing right about now, possibly falling into holes and twisting her ankle on small bits of wood. We'll find her eventually, because she'll be screaming and whimpering and not silently hiding like a smart person would."

So we're just gonna wait until we hear a scream? The mask sounded dubious.

"That's right," Larry said, smiling.

Just then, a terrified scream echoed through the woods.

Lucky bastard, said the mask.

22
Woods and a Mesh Fence – 2014

Freddy slapped a hand to Amanda's mouth, cutting her off mid-scream. "Shhhh," he said, which is what people usually say when they want other people to be quiet. Amanda bit his hand, and it was his turn to scream. It was all very *Laurel and Hardy*, but, hey, that's what the kids want, isn't it?

Staring down at the body, Amanda trembled. "It's Cedric, isn't it? The fucker killed Cedric!"

The NEVER TRUST AN ATOM, THEY MAKE UP EVERYTHING tee-shirt was a dead giveaway. It was Cedric, all right, minus a face. "It's him," Freddy said, nursing his gnawed-upon hand beneath his armpit – everyone knows that's where you put your wounds if you expect them to get better. "He looks weird without his specs."

"He never hurt a fly," Amanda said, snivelling.

Or ate one, Freddy thought but didn't say. "I don't think one of us did this."

Amanda's eyes widened. "I know *I* didn't," she said. "Where were you between the hours of nine and one tonight?"

"With *you*," Freddy said. "But I don't think any of our group did this."

"How can you be so sure?"

Freddy pointed through the trees, to what appeared to be a cabin. A large cabin. If there were several small cabins surrounding it, one might say it was a *main* cabin. Hanging from a tree branch in front of the cabin, like Christmas ornaments or Michael Hutchence after a vigorous wank, were four bodies.

Lakresha Loomis...Junior Kramer...Bailey Painter...Melissa Voorhees. The latter pair were dangling by their arms, since their heads were missing. It was a sight that would have given Tim Burton serious wood.

"Oh no!" Amanda said, doing the math in her head. "That's everyone dead except for us."

"Why are Lakresha and Junior cuffed together?" Freddy said. It was one of those things that they might never know the answer to, like *What is the meaning of life?* and *What is the purpose of Justin Bieber?*

"How did we end up back at the main cabin?" Amanda said, dropping to her knees. "What is it with these fucking woods?"

Freddy helped her back to her feet and dusted the raccoon shit off her knees. It wasn't a good look for her. "At least we know where we are, now," he said. It should have sounded comforting, but didn't. "All we have to do is retrace our steps from when we arrived at the cabin. We'll be out of here in no time."

"*Squeeeeeeeeeeee-splutter-cough-cough.* You know what? I can't make that noise anymore."

Freddy and Amanda turned just in time to see a pig-masked, bloody-aproned (nice and crisp, though), axe-wielding lunatic limp out of the trees, gasping for air, wheezing like a broken accordion. He staggered forwards, dragging the axe along the ground as if it weighed more than he could bodily manage.

"You'll have to bear with me," Pigface said, still yanking at the recalcitrant axe. "My arms have gone. It's the arthritis, see.

Runs in the family. I'll be with you in a minute. If you just want to run around for a bit, scream, maybe trip up a few times, I'll get to you as soon as possible."

Amanda grabbed hold of Freddy's arm. "It's *Pigface*," she said. "Like in the story. Jason was telling the truth. He didn't perish back in '78."

"No, I *didn't*," Pigface said, hoisting the axe up onto his shoulder. "It was touch and go there for a while, but I managed to put myself out. Suffered terrible emphysema ever since, but shouldn't complain, really."

"You killed our friends," Freddy said, not quite sure where to put himself without looking like a coward. Behind Amanda seemed like the best place.

"Oh, you noticed?" Pigface said, gesturing to the swinging bodies across the clearing. "Not my finest work, but I've got these worms, you see, and my back's about as straight as a night out in Brighton. Almost shit out my spleen lifting that jock. Would have been a lot easier if I hadn't lopped his head off. Doubt it weighed much, anyway."

Amanda screamed. It came out of nowhere, and thusly startled and terrified both Freddy and the pig-masked killer. "What?" she said, shrugging nonchalantly. "One of us had to do it."

Freddy turned his attention back to Pigface. "So now you're going to kill us? Is that how this ends?"

Pigface grunted, which was rather apt. "That's how it ends for *you*," he said. "Me...I get to go home and have a nice mug of Horlicks before bed."

"But we're not the ones who threw you in the pig-sty back in 1956," Amanda said. She was clutching at straws, but in that moment there didn't seem to be anything else to clutch at.

"Oh, *that*?" Pigface said. "I'd forgotten all *about* that. Are you kids still banging on about it after all this time? Sheesh, get a life. Got a pig of my own, now. Lovely little Angeln Saddleback. Doesn't say much, but it's better than a cat. Wilbur's his name, or *her* name, I never figured out whether it was a winkie or just a very large vulva. That's the thing about living in the woods; no local library."

Freddy didn't know how they'd managed to get onto the subject of swine anatomy, but it was buying them valuable time. If only he'd been using that time to figure out how they were going to escape this madman's clutches instead of picturing piggy private parts.

"Anyhoooo," Pigface said, testing the blade of his axe with his finger. "It's been lovely chatting, but I have to be back before morning. It's the mother, see. She'll go spare if she knows I've gone on the kill again. Funny that, isn't it?"

Amanda had heard a lot of funny things in her life. Like the time her sister had belched for over a minute, and the time she went to see Hanson on concert, but there was nothing funny about Pigface's little anecdote. Perhaps they had a different sense of humour up here, like they did in Canada...

"Well, thanks for being here," Pigface said. "It would have been shit if I'd got myself all worked up only to find the place empty."

"You're welcome," Amanda said. "But at the risk of sounding like Columbo, there is one more thing."

Pigface sighed. This was all dragging on a bit now. "Go on, then."

"Well, I'm the final girl," she said, taking a step forward, "and I'm sick and tired of running." What she wouldn't have done for a long, sharp poking stick.

"Suit yourself," Pigface said, raising his axe. "I do like a good struggle with a pretty girl." He thought about *squee*-ing, changed his mind, and was about to swing the axe when something hard, heavy, and very rocky clobbered into his temple. The hard, heavy rock thumped into the ground at his feet, and a moment later he was heading toward it. He was unconscious before he hit the ground, which was a good thing. It meant he didn't hear the mask say, *See. Too old for this shit. But you wouldn't listen, would you...I mean, why would anyone listen to a rubber pig mask? Well, I'll tell you for why...*

Freddy tugged Amanda back, away from the fallen maniac, and more importantly, away from the middle-aged woman walking across the clearing, slapping her hands together in that way people do when they're done roughing up a rival. She had a weathered face, more handsome than beautiful, like post-*Top Gun* Kelly McGillis. It was as if she hadn't even noticed Freddy and Amanda standing there. She was wholly focused on the felled lunatic, who was now snoring his little, caved-in head off.

"Help me get him inside," the woman said, prising the axe from his loose grasp. "And I hope you've got a working kettle in there." Though the last time she'd been here, the kettle had had a severed penis floating in it. "I'm parched."

23
The Main Cabin – 2014

When Pigface came to, the first thing he realised was that he couldn't move. Three rolls of duct tape will do that to a person. The second thing he realised was that he was indoors, back in the main cabin where he'd butchered the black couple. The third thing he realised was that his mask had been removed, and stared back at him from where it sat upon a table across the room. He could no longer hear what it was saying, but he had a feeling it was something along the lines of *Told you so, you geriatric tosspot.*

In the corner of the room, an electric kettle boiled, and standing beside said kettle were three people, two of whom Larry was already familiar, and a handsome lady that bore an uncanny resemblance to someone he'd met once before.

"Mine's a coffee, two sugars," Larry said. It was wrong to refer to him as Pigface now that the mask had been removed. "And then if you could undo all this tape, I'll be out of your hair in no time."

The woman stirred her drink, picked up her cup, and walked across to the middle of the room, to where Larry sat strapped to a chair. Now that he could see her face more clearly, terror surged through his body, gooseflesh rose on his skin, and the tiniest of bottom exhalations escaped, almost gassing his worms to death. The final girl from '78 had come back to haunt him, or tie him to a chair and drink coffee in front of him; one or the other.

"You," he said.

"Me," she agreed, blowing the steam from her mug. "Little Betsy Krueger, all grown up."

Larry chewed on his beard for a second, and then said, "How?"

The woman gestured to a small, flashing red light directly above the dumbstruck teenagers. "I've been waiting for this moment for thirty-six years," she said. "I knew you weren't dead the moment your remains went missing. So I waited, and waited, and then they rebuilt this place in '79, and I knew it was only a matter of time before you decided to come a-*squeeing* again. I fitted a camera. Only a cheap thing from eBay – I almost lost it to some guy called Penisbreath209 – but it does the job."

"So you've been watching all this time?" Amanda said from the corner of the room.

"Not all of it," Betsy said. "A lot of it was boring. Back in 2007, I watched two spiders mating. That was some night. Of course, I couldn't watch all the time, although in the beginning I tried. When this place was rebuilt, the camera was much bigger, and a lot harder to hide. I had a two-way mirror thing going on, but it felt a bit wrong, a bit pervy, so when technology moved forward, I was so relieved. Plus I had to come in here every few days and change the tapes, which was a logistical nightmare. Eventually I moved closer to the camp. Just down the hill, actually, and instead of watching the camera all day and all night, I had a sensor fitted to let me know when movement was detected in here. It also started the camera recording. Like I said, technology changed, and I—”

“Is this going anywhere?” Larry said. “Only I’ve got to be back before morning. Ma’s making pancakes.”

The woman – Betsy Krueger – smiled, and it was a horrible smile; more horrible even than the stitched together grin of the pig-mask watching from the table.

“She’s going to say something mean,” Freddy whispered to Amanda.

“Good,” Amanda whispered back.

“Oh, you’re not going anywhere,” Betsy said, putting down her mug and picking up the axe. “You see, I haven’t been watching for the fun of it, like *Big Brother* or *I’m a Z-List Celebrity, Feed Me Some Witchetty Grubs!*”

Larry frowned. No wonder mother didn't own a TV.

"You can close your eyes now, if you like." Betsy swung the axe back and grinned again. "This is going to sting like a bitch."

"I can't watch," Amanda said, turning away. "But I can't not watch," she added, turning back.

"Well this is a turn-up for the books," Larry said. A second later the axe came down, taking his arm off at the shoulder. It thumped to the floor, squelched as it continued to wriggle and writhe. Larry screamed, drooled, spat blood, and did other things that people do when they've just lost an appendage. "You *bitch*!" he yelled. "You heartless *bitch*!"

Betsy moved across so that she was level with the other arm. "Heartless?" she said. "After what you did to my friends...to *their* friends." She poked the axe toward Amanda and Freddy; Amanda and Freddy both took a step back. "You ought to be ashamed of yourself."

"I am," Larry lied. "Extremely. Now, if you could leave me with one good arm, that would be—" He didn't get to finish the sentence before his other arm was sliced clear of his body. "Aaaaaaagh! You're a maniac! A damned *lunatic*! I was going to take up jigsaw puzzles, you *cunt*!"

"I hate that word," Betsy said. "Pu-*zzles*. Sounds like a wasp having a seizure." She swung the axe back and slammed it into Larry's shin. He squealed, "You motherfucking evil *bitch*! Ma's going to kill me when I come home without arms and legs!" With a bit of wriggling and elbow-grease, everything from the knee down came away. Blood geysered everywhere, giving the cabin floor a good coating of crimson gloss.

"Should we *do* something?" Amanda said.

"You're right," Freddy said, reaching up to the cupboard above the kettle. "I swear Bailey brought some popcorn with him."

"Four limbs," she said, swinging the axe one more time. This one thumped into his flesh just above the left kneecap. He drooled, his head fell forward, but there was no scream this time. "One for each of the friends you took from me back in '78." She would have removed his fingers and ears first, for the twelve nonentities that had also perished, but it sounded like an awful lot of work.

"You'll suffer...for...this..." Larry mumbled through a mouthful of blood. "I...promise..." Had he known those would be his final words, perhaps he would have opted for something more memorable. It was hardly *Et tu, Brute?* was it?

Betsy Krueger, no longer smiling, said, "We've all suffered enough," and brought the axe around in a wide arc. It made a noise that...well, you know what kind of noise a swinging thing makes. It thunked! – yes *thunked*! – into Larry's neck, and his head toppled backwards off his shoulders.

"*Squeee-gargle...!*" Larry said as his head rolled along the floorboards, leaving a trail of blood in its wake.

Freddy stopped pushing popcorn into his mouth and said, "Well that escalated quickly." And then, "Holy shit! Some fucker's broken my guitar!"

Betsy Krueger dropped the axe and walked to where her coffee was going cold. She picked it up and sipped at it, thoughtfully, before saying. "It isn't over yet. We have to burn the place down, burn his body like I should have all those years ago."

Amanda nodded. "I'll get the matches."

Freddy vomited. "Bluergh, that snuck up on me," he said. On the bright side, he didn't have to mop it up, not if they were going to torch the place.

And so there was petrol, and fire, and melting rubber, and burning flesh, and ashes, and bits of things floating through the air, getting in the mouths of those not paying attention. From the woods, an owl watched, shaking its head and saying *hooooo*. It was a told-you-so *hooooo*, not that any of the survivors spoke owl to know that. There was crackling and hissing and thankfully no *squee*-ing as the cabin burnt to the ground. The bodies were brought down from the tree out front and placed on the fire, though placed was not quite the right word for it. *Launched*, now *that* was the right word.

"I can give you a ride into town, if you like," Betsy said. "It's sixty miles away, but that's the thing with these camps, isn't it? So damn far away from civilisation. No wonder they keep attracting the nut-jobs."

"Thanks," Amanda said. "It'll give us a chance to figure out what just happened. Does this town have a police station?"

"It has a *sheriff*," Betsy said, "but he drinks...a *lot*. He's just finished dealing with some haunted house murders over in Amityville. You'd be better off telling it to the newspapers, but if I were you, I'd just forget about it. Move on. Put it behind you. Hope there isn't a sequel."

"Probably for the best," Amanda said. "We all know the final girl gets it in the opening scene of the sequel."

"There's no way he could have survived *that*," Freddy said. The cabin collapsed and hissed and continued to burn; it couldn't have happened at a better time if someone was writing it, making it up as they went along.

"No, of *course* not," Betsy said, glancing nervously at Amanda, who turned to glance nervously at Freddy, who turned to find there was nobody for him to nervously glance at, and he didn't want to set the whole thing going again so he glanced at the ground.

"Let's get out of here," Amanda said.

"Damn *straight*," Freddy said.

"Right behind you," Betsy said, though she wasn't. She was leading the way, if anything. It was almost a race to Betsy's car – a battered old Plymouth Fury in race-car red. "Don't mind Cujo," she said, gesturing to the huge dog taking up most of the passenger seat. "He doesn't bite, but he has been acting a little strangely recently. Ever since we found those bats in the garden."

"You know what?" Freddy said, stopping in front of the car, which appeared to be giving off some kind of bad vibe. He took Amanda by the hand. She gave it a little squeeze to let him know that she was thinking the same thing.

"I think we'll walk," they said in unison. It was cheesy, like the ending of some crappy video-nasty from the eighties, but there you go. If this were a film or a book, you wouldn't pay more than three bucks for it, and if you would, well, more fool you...

Epilogue
Larry II? Really? You're Shitting me!

The old lady sifted through the rubble, tossing bits of wood aside, and cursing under her breath every time she came across a piece of her beloved son that wasn't reduced to ash. An arm here, a leg there, burnt but not indiscernible, although a couple of them were blacker than her son's had been, and she was pretty sure he didn't have a tattoo of a pink butterfly on his shoulder. She bagged them all anyway – it was a *bag-for-life,* which meant that it was already buckling from the weight – and pushed on further into the wooden ruins.

"Don't listen to your old ma," she mumbled. "Think you know it all. Well ya *don't.* Ya don't know *shit.*" She leaned over, grabbed a piece of still-smoking wood, and threw it aside, revealing something pink, something partially melted. Something awfully *porcine.*

With a bit of effort – and it was a bit, which, for an almost-centenarian, wasn't bad at all – Edie Travers managed to free the mask from the smouldering pile. "Well, suck me sideways," she said. The mask was entirely melted on one side, but the other side was fine, untouched, if not a little grubby. She dropped it into the bag with the six arms and three legs and clambered down from the ashes and remains of what used to be a perfectly good cabin.

"Shoulda listened to me, Larry," she moaned plaintively as the woods swallowed her up. "Shoulda done the puzzles. Shoulda played the bingo. Shoulda taken up pipe-smoking and Sudokus."

She was halfway home when she could have sworn she heard a voice. Just a small thing, almost inaudible, actually, but a mouthful of severed limbs would do that to a pig-mask.

Writing it off as dementia, the old lady continued into the trees, of which, as you're well aware by now, there were many, but that was the thing about woods. Sometimes you couldn't see the trees for them.

www.ingramcontent.com/pod-product-compliance
Lightning Source LLC
Chambersburg PA
CBHW011137190726
48289CB00012B/3068